"I'm aware of the fact that I'm attracted to you."

She handed him his jacket as she continued, "I just don't intend to do anything about it."

"I'm going to keep working on you until you give in."

Charly turned away from him. "Don't think today was a taste of what's to come. I have always been in control of my actions." *Until now,* a voice mocked.

"Then you've slipped up badly tonight," Aaron taunted. "Now that I've seen what it's like between us, I'm not going to make do with anything less than all of you. And I've never given up on anything I wanted as badly as I want you. Matt may be my best friend, but he's going to find himself ousted from your life so quickly that he'll wonder if he was ever in it." He leaned forward and kissed her. "I want your complete surrender."

Books by Carole Mortimer

HARLEQUIN PRESENTS
571—PERFECT PARTNER
579—GOLDEN FEVER
587—HIDDEN LOVE
594—LOVE'S ONLY DECEPTION
603—CAPTIVE LOVING
611—FANTASY GIRL
619—HEAVEN HERE ON EARTH
627—LIFELONG AFFAIR
636—LOVE UNSPOKEN
645—UNDYING LOVE
651—SUBTLE REVENGE
659—PAGAN ENCHANTMENT
669—TRUST IN SUMMER MADNESS
675—THE FAILED MARRIAGE
684—SENSUAL ENCOUNTER
716—EVERLASTING LOVE
724—HARD TO GET
740—A LOST LOVE
757—UNTAMED
773—AN UNWILLING DESIRE
780—A PAST REVENGE
786—THE PASSIONATE LOVER
797—TEMPESTUOUS AFFAIR
804—CHERISH TOMORROW
812—A NO RISK AFFAIR
829—LOVERS IN THE AFTERNOON
852—THE DEVIL'S PRICE
860—LADY SURRENDER

These books may be available at your local bookseller.

Don't miss any of our special offers. Write to us at the
following address for information on our newest releases.

Harlequin Reader Service
P.O. Box 52040, Phoenix, AZ 85072-2040
Canadian address: P.O. Box 2800, Postal Station A,
5170 Yonge St., Willowdale, Ont. M2N 6J3

CAROLE MORTIMER

lady surrender

Harlequin Books

TORONTO • NEW YORK • LONDON
AMSTERDAM • PARIS • SYDNEY • HAMBURG
STOCKHOLM • ATHENS • TOKYO • MILAN

For John,
Matthew and Joshua

Harlequin Presents first edition February 1986
ISBN 0-373-10860-5

Original hardcover edition published in 1985
by Mills & Boon Limited

CHAPTER ONE

CHARLY barely had time to click back the lock on the apartment door before it was pushed forcibly open, knocking her off-balance as she grabbed at the towel she had quickly draped about herself when the doorbell rang seconds ago, having to get out of the shower to answer it.

The man who had pushed his way in towered over her five foot frame, but there was still challenge in her wide grey eyes as she looked up at him, successfully hiding her nervousness at this intrusion. 'I don't know who you are——'

'No,' he acknowledged harshly. 'But I know who you are!' His aggressive accent was definitely American.

'Obviously,' she drawled. 'If you're after money or jewellery I think I should tell you I don't have any here.'

His green-eyed gaze raked over her contemptuously. 'Women like you only have one jewel, lady, and even that gets tarnished after a while.'

Charly gasped at the crude insult, all nervousness fading. 'If you want to take what valuables there are then do so and leave,' she instructed haughtily.

His mouth twisted. 'You're pretty free with what doesn't belong to you, aren't you?' he scorned derisively. 'But then you have no idea of morality, do you?'

'I beg your pardon!' She raised light brown

brows indignantly, their indistinctive colour making it difficult to tell whether the hair beneath the second towel she had draped around her wet hair was blonde, brunette, or auburn, or a mixture of all three.

'I'm not the one you should be apologising to——'

'Are you some sort of political fanatic?' Charly frowned suspiciously.

'Hell, no!'

'Then what do you want? If it's me, I ought to tell you I've been taught self-defence.'

'Lady, I wouldn't care if you were a judo and Kung Fu expert rolled into one,' he dismissed harshly. 'I'm not about to let a five foot nothing woman defeat me in achieving what I came here to do!'

As he must have stood about six foot four, was deeply muscled beneath the pale green shirt and leather jacket, his legs lean and strong beneath black trousers, and her self-defence classes had been nowhere near as expert as judo or Kung Fu, he could be right! But she wasn't about to let him know that. 'My husband is in the bedroom,' she told him firmly, hoping the classical lie in a situation like this sounded more convincing to him than it did to her.

The green eyes became contemptuous. 'You don't have a husband of your own, only someone else's—and I happen to know he's out of town!'

Charly gave an irritated frown. 'Are you sure you have the right apartment?' Maybe they could laugh together about this once he realised his mistake— but she doubted it. This man was beyond a joke, and the situation wasn't at all funny!

In other circumstances she might even have thought him attractive. He had a certain rakish appearance, casually styled black hair, a reckless light in those deep green eyes, his mouth firmly sculptured, his jaw square, his lean body obviously kept in physical health, although the cynicism in his expression wasn't quite as attractive, or the derision for her he didn't try to hide behind politeness.

'This is Matt Parker's apartment, isn't it?' he rasped.

'Yes,' she frowned.

'And you are Charly, aren't you?'

She stiffened. 'Only my friends are allowed to call me that.'

He gave her a contemptuous look. 'And I'm sure there are a lot of them, honey—all male!'

She drew in an angry breath. 'I don't know if you mean to be insulting——'

'Oh, I do,' he drawled. 'Believe me, I do!'

'You don't know the first thing about me——'

'I know the *only* thing I want to know about you,' he scoffed. 'Matt must have been insane to get mixed up with a woman like you.' He looked at her critically. 'Admittedly, you're beautiful——'

'Thank you!' she said with sarcasm.

'In an earthy sort of way.' His gaze lingered on the pert fullness of her breasts and the generous curve of her hips. 'But you certainly don't look worth throwing away eight years of marriage, a lovely wife, and two kids for!' he added scathingly.

'I'm sure you're right——'

'You bet I am. And when Matt gets back from

this damned trip he's going to thank me for finishing things between you—after I've killed him,' he muttered grimly. 'I did enough bailing out for him at university; I don't expect to still have to do it!'

Charly was more puzzled than ever. 'You were at university with Matt?'

'Yes. Now when Molly gets here I want you to——'

'Matt's wife is coming here?' She frowned her confusion. 'Whatever for?'

'Don't act dumb,' he scowled. 'Or maybe you are,' he derided. 'A mistress doesn't usually answer the telephone in her lover's apartment and speak to his wife! Unless you're trying to break them up?' he grated. 'You don't fancy being the next Mrs Matt Parker, do you?' he scorned. 'Believe me, it will never happen. Matt may be infatuated with you at the moment, but he'll listen to me when I tell him you're nothing but a mercenary little tramp.'

Charly had a feeling much like it must be to be run over by a steam-roller! 'I'm sure he will,' she answered dazedly.

He nodded, as if there were no doubting the fact. 'In the meantime we have to convince Molly that she's all wrong about the two of you.'

'And just how do you propose to do that?' she asked dryly.

'With the only language women like you understand—money,' he told her derisively.

Charly stiffened, resentment in every bone of her body. 'Is that so?' she drawled.

He nodded, his expression contemptuous. 'And a little acting on your part too—but I'm sure that won't be difficult for you either,' he dismissed with disgust.

In other circumstances she would have put this man firmly in his place, and friend of Matt's or not, it would not have been this apartment! But at the moment she was too bemused—certainly not *amused!*—by the assumption he seemed to have made about her and Matt. She was even more interested in hearing how he intended dealing with the situation.

'Go on,' she invited.

'I've told Molly that you're my girlfriend.' The man looked at her with dislike.

Charly returned that dislike—with interest. 'Couldn't you have thought of something better than *that*?'

'In the thinking time I had, *no*,' he glared at her. 'I got in to the country yesterday——'

'I guessed you weren't English,' she scorned.

'Not gentlemanly enough for you, hmm?' he derided. 'Well I don't know where you got that plummy accent from,' he dismissed harshly, 'but I can assure you I don't think of you as a lady either!'

Insulting man! Her parents had paid a small fortune for her to acquire this 'plummy accent'. And she didn't think it was 'plummy' at all, just correct English. Ignorant lout!

'You were telling me about this marvellous plan you had devised to convince Molly that Matt and I aren't lovers,' she prompted in a bored voice. 'And perhaps it would be better if you introduced yourself.'

Green eyes glittered dangerously. 'The name is

Aaron Grantley. And I'd advise you not to irritate me, lady; I'm angry enough already!'

The threat passed unheeded. Aaron Grantley! She had had no idea what he looked like and so hadn't recognised him, although he was much more well-known in his native America. But she had heard of him, knew that when it came to business there was none better, that the man had amassed a fortune and a hotel empire in America using his business acumen, that he was now interested in advancing into England. Charly hadn't realised he was in the country. Perhaps she ought to put an end to this right now, before——

'Women like you are a dime a dozen,' he told her coldly. 'Damn parasites, living off the vulnerability of married men——'

'Mr Grantley——'

'Believe me, the thought of having to pretend to be your lover makes my skin crawl,' he added disgustedly. 'You would have to get me so damned drunk I wouldn't know what I was doing before I could make love to you!' he bit out insultingly. 'But I'm sure there are lots of men who aren't averse to paying for your services, one way or another.'

Charly was very pale by the time he had finished, all idea of denying a relationship with Matt completely forgotten. Even if she were the sort of woman this man thought she was he had no right to talk to her in this way. People who knew her well would have recognised and understood the anger in silver eyes that were usually a calm grey, and they would have very wisely not pushed her any further.

'I believe you mentioned something about money yourself,' she prompted hardly.

The firmly sculptured mouth twisted derisively. 'I didn't think you would have missed that.'

She gave a haughty inclination of her head. 'I never ignore the mention of money, Mr Grantley.'

He nodded. 'I already guessed that,' he drawled. 'I'm prepared to pay you well to pretend to be my girlfriend while Molly is here.'

'How much?'

'I see the thought of money puts colour in your cheeks,' he scorned harshly.

If there were any colour in her cheeks it was anger at this man. How dare he come here making assumptions, throwing out accusations and insults! She might regret her silence later, but for the moment she relished the time she would tell this man how wrong he was.

'I said how much, Mr Grantley?' she repeated coldly.

He gave a disgusted snort. 'I bet Matt has never seen you like this; I'm sure you're always sweet and lovable with him!'

Charly looked at him steadily. 'I have no reason not to be,' she stated truthfully.

'I suppose he bought you those little rocks.' Aaron Grantley glared at the diamond studs in her earlobes.

'Actually, no,' she told him smoothly.

'Then some other poor besotted idiot did,' he accused disgustedly.

James had never been poor, and certainly not a besotted idiot, she thought bitterly. 'What sort of

payment did you have in mind, Mr Grantley?'
she asked him hardly.

'How about a bracelet to match the earrings?'

Her brows rose; whatever this man was he
wasn't miserly! 'Your friendship with Matt must
be a very close one,' she frowned.

'Not close enough, obviously.' His gaze raked
over her contemptuously. 'He certainly didn't tell
me about you.' He made the statement an insult.

Charly shrugged. 'Probably because he knew
you would disapprove.'

'Any real friend would,' he rasped. 'The
damned fool is married!'

'Are you married?' She didn't remember ever
hearing about any marriage, but it was always a
possibility.

His mouth twisted. 'My marital state is none of
your business!'

'I just thought, with Molly being a friend, you
might find—this—awkward, if you have a wife
too.'

Aaron Grantley sighed. 'I don't have a wife, a
live-in girlfriend, or indeed any serious relationship at the moment. Which is just as well
with Matt in this mess,' he ground out.

She nodded. 'You had better tell me exactly
what you've told Molly about us.'

'Not a lot,' he grated forcefully. 'How could I
when I knew nothing about you? Matt had
mentioned to me that this apartment wouldn't be
available for my stay because he was letting
Charly stay here for a while; I assumed it was one
of his colleagues from the hospital that he lets use
it when it isn't convenient for them to travel out
of town to their homes. He also told Molly that

someone was using the apartment before he left yesterday but he didn't say who, and like me she assumed it was one of his colleagues from the hospital. Then she realised Matt had left an address book here that she needed, and telephoned to see if this colleague could send it on to her. You answered the telephone,' he accused.

Charly vaguely remembered the hastily ended conversation with a woman caller earlier, the other woman ringing off once she was told Charly wasn't the doctor on duty at the hospital that evening. Charly hadn't thought anything of it at the time, now she realised that must have been Molly.

'The poor woman is worried out of her mind,' Aaron Grantley told her harshly. 'She's left the kids with her mother and is driving up here immediately.'

Charly frowned. 'And where do you come in to it, besides being Matt's friend?'

'Molly telephoned me after talking to you, to invite me down to dinner tomorrow, and also to ask me if I knew anything about you—casually. Too casually,' he added pointedly.

'You're having dinner with Matt's wife while he's away?' she taunted.

His mouth tightened formidably. 'He'll be back tomorrow afternoon; don't credit everyone else with your alley-cat morals!'

She drew in an angry breath. 'If you're so damned pure why does Molly believe you're capable of keeping a woman at your best friend's apartment?' she accused coldly.

'Doesn't the fact that she's driving up here anyway tell you that she doesn't believe it?' His eyes glittered. 'She knows damn well I would do anything to protect Matt, and that includes lying for him. So you had better give the performance of your life, lady!'

'How do you know I don't work at the hospital?' she frowned. 'They have allowed women to enter professions for some years now, you know,' she added scornfully.

'Molly knows the names of the people Matt lets stay here, and none of them are called Charly! Besides,' he looked at her derisively, 'you don't look as if you have the brains to do more than entertain a man!'

A chauvinist as well as everything else! 'I'm not surprised you don't have a woman in your life at the moment, Mr Grantley,' she bit out coldly. 'In fact, I'm surprised you've *ever* had one with your opinion of us!'

'How do you think I came by this opinion?' he scorned.

She looked him over coolly. 'By choosing the wrong sort of woman, obviously. But they were probably the only sort *you* could get! Certainly no intelligent woman would want to be involved with such a male chauvinist.'

'Pig,' he finished derisively. 'That is the colloquialism of today, isn't it?' he drawled at her questioning look.

'Male chauvinistic pig,' she tested the statement for sound. 'Yes, I believe that applies to you quite nicely.'

'And we both know my opinion of you,' he rasped. 'So my acting had better be good too!'

'Just when are you expecting Molly to arrive?'

'It takes just over an hour from the house, so

any time now, I would think,' he scowled. 'So you had better get yourself dressed.'

'Wouldn't it look more convincing if I stayed as I am?' she mocked.

Cold green eyes looked her over critically. 'Get dressed,' he instructed abruptly. 'There's no reason for us to look as if we've just been to bed together.'

'Heaven forbid it should look as if you had actually made love to me!' Her eyes flashed.

'How old are you?' he rasped.

'Twenty-six,' she was surprised into answering the question. 'What does that have to do with anything?'

His mouth twisted. 'I would have thought that by now you would have been used to the knocks.'

Her expression became unreadable. 'I am,' she answered abruptly. 'I just don't expect insults from a man I don't even know—and who certainly doesn't know me,' she added hardly.

'What I do know I don't like,' he bit out. 'But you had better tell me a little about yourself so that this act at least stands a chance of succeeding.'

'My name is Charly—Allenby, I'm unmarried, and as I've already told you, I'm twenty-six.'

Aaron Grantley frowned darkly. 'That's all?'

'The prisoner is only required to give name, rank, and number,' she drawled derisively.

'Stop being so damned blasé,' he rasped grimly. 'I'm trying to save the marriage of my two dearest friends—and you're being paid to help me!'

'Maybe if you didn't make assumptions——'

'The next thing I know you'll be claiming that

your being here is perfectly innocent,' he scorned.

'It is. Look, why would Matt tell you or his wife I were here if I were his mistress?'

'He told Molly because he didn't want her to come here and find you in residence, and he told me for the same reason. Charly, go and get some clothes on,' he said wearily. 'You're just wasting time.'

She had never met anyone like him, even James hadn't been this arrogant! 'If you'll just let me explain——'

'I don't want to hear all the details,' he snapped, settling himself down in an armchair. 'After tonight I don't even want to see you again.'

She sighed. 'I don't suppose it's of any interest to you that I was going out this evening?'

'None at all,' he confirmed flatly. 'And remember, as far as you're concerned Molly is merely coming here to collect an address book; don't embarrass her by letting her know you're aware of the real reason.'

She left the room after giving him an indignant glare. Living with James' arrogance had been frustrating enough, accepting a far deeper arrogance from a complete stranger was un-acceptable to her.

But he wasn't a *complete* stranger. She had heard all too much of Aaron Grantley in the business world during recent weeks, his latest business venture even intruding into her life. And now the man himself had come bursting into her life with the same intrusive determination to get what he wanted. Well he was going to get far more than he had bargained for from her tonight!

She was putting the finishing touches to her hair when she heard the doorbell ring, turning off the dryer to hear the murmur of voices in the lounge, a breathless female one, and Aaron Grantley's softer soothing one. She hoped his acting ability was as good as he seemed confident it was, because he was going to need it during the next few seconds!

The couple in the lounge weren't initially aware of her presence, and she took the opportunity to watch Molly unobserved. She was a tall, pretty woman, about Charly's own age, with short black hair, darkly lashed blue eyes, talking worriedly to Aaron Grantley. They both seemed to become aware of Charly's presence at the same moment, turning simultaneously.

It was lucky for Aaron Grantley that the other woman did turn to look at her too, because his mouth literally fell open as he gazed at Charly in dazed surprise. She had been well aware of the impact she would make, had dressed with just that idea in mind. The black and gold dress was Japanese in style, high-necked, short-sleeved, completely figure-hugging, her legs long and shapely beneath its knee length, her gold sandals adding to her height with three-inch heels. Her hair was a straight golden swathe to her waist, her make-up dark and dramatic, far heavier than she normally wore it. Aaron Grantley could now see exactly why a man, married or otherwise, could lose his head over her!

'I hope I wasn't too long, darling.' She swayed gracefully into the room, putting her arms about his neck to kiss him lingeringly on the mouth as he stood perfectly still, rigid with shock. 'And

you must be Molly.' She turned to the other
woman, smiling warmly. 'Matt has told me so
much about you.'

Molly looked taken aback. 'I—He has?'

'Oh yes. And your two adorable children. It
was so kind of him to let me use his apartment
like this.' She glared hardly at Aaron Grantley
before moving out of his arms. 'Did you find
your address book?' she smiled at the other
woman once again.

'Er—yes.' Molly looked uncomfortable.

'Oh good,' she nodded. 'I hope it doesn't
inconvenience you that I'm staying here; the fire
just about gutted my lounge, although the
decorators hope to be finished soon. Shall we sit
down?' she invited smoothly.

Molly plopped down on to the sofa while
Charly sank down more gracefully, the length of
the slit up the skirt of her dress revealing most of
her thigh as she crossed one knee over the other.

'Fire?' Molly prompted.

'Mm,' Charly nodded, turning curiously to
Aaron Grantley as he stood across the room still
staring at her. 'Darling, why don't you sit down,'
her voice lowered throatily. 'I'm sure Molly
doesn't have to rush off.'

'I—I think I'll have a drink first,' he spoke
decisively. 'Ladies?' he added abruptly, as if he
had just remembered his manners.

They both declined, and Charly turned to
Molly as she guessed the other woman was still
waiting for an answer to her question. 'I detest
smoking at the best of times,' she confided,
having to choke back a laugh as she saw the gold
cigarette case Aaron Grantley had been reaching

for drop back unopened into the breast-pocket of the pale green shirt. 'But now I refuse to have it anywhere near me,' she added firmly, all humour gone. 'A guest at my apartment the other evening forgot about a cigarette she had been smoking and it fell beneath the coffee-table. It smouldered there until I'd gone to bed and then the carpet caught fire.'

'Oh how awful,' Molly was genuinely disturbed. 'Were you hurt?'

'I inhaled a lot of smoke before a neighbour broke down the door,' she revealed abruptly, very aware of how intently Aaron Grantley was listening now. 'They kept me in hospital for observation but I was fine.'

Molly looked accusingly at Aaron Grantley. 'You didn't tell me any of this.'

'Actually, I didn't tell him,' Charly explained truthfully. 'I knew he wouldn't have liked my having the dinner party while he wasn't here; he can be so jealous,' she confided indulgently, studiously avoiding his furious gaze.

'Aaron can?' Molly looked stunned.

'Oh yes,' Charly nodded. 'Besides, there was nothing he could do in America.'

'Then Matt should have told me about it,' Molly muttered uncomfortably.

'It only happened at the weekend,' Charly excused. 'And now that Aaron is here I can forget all about it,' she added mockingly, looking up at him challengingly.

Molly shook her head. 'The two of you seem so close, and yet Aaron hasn't breathed a word about you to us.'

'Aaron's not used to our relationship himself

yet,' she confided. 'I'm afraid he's still a little
wary of the speed with which we fell in love.'

Molly's eyes widened at this information. 'Are
the two of you engaged?' she gasped.

'I——'

'Aaron is a little too old for an engagement,'
Charly dismissed lightly, meeting his furious gaze
innocently. 'So we've just decided to get
married.' She kept her face straight as Aaron
almost choked on his whisky, his face going red
with anger.

'When?' Molly squeaked.

'Well we haven't actually decided on a date yet,
but——'

'But you can be sure you and Matt will be the
first to know when we do decide on one,' Aaron
put in forcefully. 'I thought that was going to
remain our secret for a while?' he added gratingly
to Charly.

She raised innocent brows. 'Surely not from
such good friends as Molly and Matt?'

'From anybody.' He sounded as if he were
spitting nails!

'Well, you didn't tell me that, darling,' she
drawled, relaxing back in her chair, her grey eyes
meeting his calmly. 'I'm sorry if I've ruined your
surprise.'

He looked as if that 'surprise' might have
pushed him to breaking point, although somehow
he maintained his control. 'It doesn't matter,' he
dismissed abruptly.

'I'm so glad you told me.' Molly smiled, all
doubts obviously laid to rest with this announcement. 'Matt is going to be pleased too.' She
turned to Charly. 'I invited Aaron down to

dinner tomorrow evening before I realised how seriously involved the two of you are; please come too, Charly.'

'Fine,' Aaron Grantley accepted abruptly. 'We'll look forward to it, won't we, honey?'

He was getting his revenge now! 'Yes,' she agreed curtly. 'We will.'

'Good.' Molly seemed relieved that the meeting had turned out so differently from what she had been expecting.

'Would you like some coffee before you leave?' Charly offered warmly, liking the other woman and her courage to want to fight for her husband if she had to.

'That would be nice, thank you,' Molly nodded acceptance.

'I'll help you, Charly,' Aaron Grantley put in hardly, following her from the room, swinging her round to face him once they reached the privacy of the kitchen. 'What game do you think you're playing?' he demanded furiously.

She glared up at him, shaking off his hand on her arm. 'I'm not playing at all, Mr Grantley,' she snapped. 'Your manners since you arrived here this evening have been highly insulting, to say the least. You prejudged Matt and I——'

'Molly may have fallen for that fire and smoke inhalation story, Miss Allenby,' he ground out, 'but don't expect me to be as gullible!'

'What would it take to convince you?' she demanded angrily. 'Third degree burns?'

His mouth twisted. 'I already know there aren't any; I've seen sixty per cent of you, remember?'

'You're right, Mr Grantley,' she told him

flatly. 'There are no burns.' She couldn't tell this man of the way she woke in the night, her body bathed in perspiration as she imagined that choking smoke filled her bedroom once more and she couldn't get out.

It had only been the quick action of her neighbour that had saved her from death. She had taken a sleeping tablet as usual before she went to bed that night, hadn't been aware of any danger until Jeff Pearce dragged her through the smoke-filled apartment to safety.

'I know that,' Aaron Grantley scorned. 'But it was a good story. Molly certainly believed it. It's this idea of marriage between us that you've given Molly that I don't like,' he scowled, the green eyes dark.

Charly looked up at him unblinkingly. 'I thought it was a nice touch,' she drawled.

'You realise you've put us both in an awkward position?' he rasped.

'Us?' she raised her brows, shaking her head. 'I've put *you* in an awkward position; I have no intention of going to Matt's for dinner tomorrow. You'll have to make my excuses to them.'

He gave her a contemptuous look. 'You're right; I doubt Matt has the nerve to carry out an evening with his wife *and* his mistress.'

Charly gave him a pitying look. 'I'm sure you would have more bravado,' she scorned. 'Now shouldn't you go and keep your guest company; the coffee is almost ready.'

He nodded impatiently. 'But no more wise-cracks about us getting married,' he warned.

'Or?' she drawled.

'Wait and see.' He gave a humourless smile,

challenge in the narrowed green eyes. 'You look like a woman who would like surprises,' he taunted before rejoining Molly in the lounge.

There hadn't been many surprises in her life, even fewer of them pleasant ones, while the shocks she had received in recent years had been even less pleasant. It seemed, from Aaron Grantley's viewpoint at least, that the outer shell had faired far better than the inner Charly; he certainly didn't believe there had been a fire in her apartment. He would be even more sceptical about the rest of her life!

Molly was very relaxed as she drank her coffee, her mind obviously at rest now about her husband's involvement with Charly. For all that she disliked Aaron Grantley Charly was glad they had managed to do that; it had been the only reason she had agreed to go along with Aaron Grantley's plan. No woman should have to go through the torture of believing her husband had another woman when it wasn't true; it was hard enough to bear when it was true!

'You will let us know when you decide about the wedding, won't you?' Molly prompted eagerly. 'I know Matt wouldn't want to miss the great event; for years he's been saying he doubted Aaron would ever marry,' the other woman teasingly explained to Charly. 'I'm sure he has no idea how serious your relationship is.'

'It came as a surprise to us all,' Aaron Grantley drawled derisively.

'Oh yes.' Charly put her hand in the crook of his arm, leaning into him as they sat on the sofa together. 'But now that I've managed to get a commitment from him I'm going to hang on to him.' She looked at him challengingly as she felt him stiffen.

'There's no rush,' he muttered, giving her a fierce glare.

'Neither of us is getting any younger, Aaron,' she lightly mocked.

'Thirty-five isn't old,' he grated.

'It is for a first marriage,' she drawled. 'Not so long ago people would have thought there was something wrong with you,' she added tauntingly.

His hand covered hers as it rested on his arm, crushing down on her fingers in a gesture that, to an observer, must look loving. 'We both know how wrong that assumption would be about me,' he ground out between clenched teeth, his eyes blazing with anger. 'Don't we?' His hand was even more painful on her fingers.

'Well, of course we do, darling,' she gave him a coy smile, triumph in her eyes that she had managed to unnerve him once again. 'I was merely pointing out that we shouldn't delay the wedding too much longer.'

His mouth tightened ominously. 'I don't believe in rushing into these things.'

She gave a light laugh. 'We wouldn't be rushing into anything. I don't——' her next taunt was cut off by angrily firm lips descending roughly on to hers, the brief contact of Aaron Grantley's mouth showing her just how furious he was. It was the first time she had known such intimacy from a man since——

'I think it's time I left,' Molly gently teased, standing up. 'I hope you didn't mind my collecting the address book.' Once again she avoided Charly's gaze. 'I—I'll see you both tomorrow.'

'I——'

'Yes, we'll be there,' Aaron cut in firmly, not wanting to give her the chance to say anything that might be even more damning, standing up to join Molly at the door. 'Tell Matt I'll call him tomorrow.'

'So will I,' Charly put in determinedly, making no effort to join them as Aaron saw the other woman to the lift.

She was standing in front of the window trying to decide how she felt about that kiss when she sensed he had come back into the room. She didn't actually have a lot to compare his kiss with, certainly hadn't been expecting it, or he could have been deeply embarrassed by her violent recoil from the caress. She finally decided she didn't *know* how she felt about the kiss.

'You will not call Matt tomorrow or at any other time,' Aaron ground out icily.

She straightened her shoulders, her expression cold as she turned to face him. 'I won't?' she drawled.

'No,' he rasped. 'You've had your fun here tonight, but now it's over. I want you to pack your things and move out of here right now.'

'And where would I go?'

'Find some other fool to support you in the life to which you've become accustomed,' he scorned. 'I really don't care where you go—just do it.'

She shrugged. 'Matt isn't going to be too pleased about this.'

Aaron Grantley scowled. 'Matt will soon realise what an idiot he's been!'

'You think so?' she frowned thoughtfully.

'I know so,' he said contemptuously.

'You probably know him better than I do,' she nodded consideringly. 'But I have no intention of moving out of here tonight.'

'Now look, lady——'

'Will you stop calling me "lady" in that contemptuous tone,' she snapped coldly. 'We both know you consider me to be the opposite!'

He looked at her with narrowed eyes, his lashes a sooty black against the green depths. 'With that damned haughty manner of yours you could find yourself an earl or something, why pick on Matt?'

'He's a very eminent doctor——'

'But hardly jet-set material.'

Her mouth twisted scornfully. 'I'm not interested in the so-called jet-set,' she dismissed. 'I like my men intelligent as well as interesting; Matt is both of those things,' she added pointedly.

'Implying I'm not?'

Her brows rose coolly. 'I thought the idea was for me not to find you attractive?' she mocked.

He drew in a ragged breath. 'It is!'

She looked at him with derision. 'And I can assure you I don't.'

'I'll make your excuses to Molly and Matt tomorrow,' he ground out. 'You just make sure you're gone from here before Matt comes up to town again.'

'And if I'm not?'

'You don't have the diamond bracelet yet, Charly,' he reminded harshly. 'Something Matt, for all his ability as a doctor, isn't able to buy for you.'

Something snapped inside her, a rage towards him and other arrogant men like him. 'I don't want your bracelet, Mr Grantley,' she bit out tautly. 'I helped you out tonight because—because I know how Molly must be feeling at this moment.'

'Been replaced a few times yourself, have you?' he derided contemptuously.

She flushed fiery red in her anger. 'As a matter of fact, *yes*!'

He nodded. 'Small, chubby blondes aren't exactly in fashion at the moment, are they?'

'I may be small and blonde, but I am certainly not chubby,' Charly snapped.

'Well-endowed?' he taunted.

'Curvaceous,' she bit out, thinking how ridiculous this conversation had become. 'I don't have the time for this,' she claimed grimly. 'I had an appointment half an hour ago; I'd like to get there soon.'

'I don't have the time to waste either,' he rasped. 'Some rich bitch is trying to buy my deal from under me, and I consider that a hell of a lot more important than arguing with you!'

She raised light brown brows with practised calm. 'Aren't you rich yourself, Mr Grantley?' she drawled mockingly.

'I worked for what I have,' he said harshly. 'I didn't have it handed to me with my gold spoon.'

'I believe the saying is "*silver* spoon",' she corrected softly.

'Not in this case,' he scorned grimly. 'It's been gold for Rocharlle Hart from day one. She was born into money, married money, and now she's trying to use some of that money to ruin a property deal I badly want.'

'Maybe Mrs Hart wants it as badly,' Charly derided his arrogance.

'Women like her don't have wants or needs,' he dismissed roughly. 'Only a quest for power.'

'You don't sound as if you've ever met her, so how can you know——'

'I *know*,' he cut in firmly. 'Just as I know you aren't going to see Matt again.'

'That might be a little difficult——'

'I could make things very unpleasant for you if you don't agree to this.'

His threat only angered her more. 'Mr Grantley, perhaps there's something you should know——'

'About you?' he scorned. 'I don't think so.'

'You might regret not listening to me,' she suggested with soft emphasis.

'I doubt that.'

She shrugged. 'It's important.'

'Just as making sure you have varnish on your toenails is important to you, no doubt!' he looked contemptuously at the offending toenails, the varnish the same deep shade as her fingernails. 'You look like a damned slave-girl!'

'Is it a crime to want to look nice?' she snapped defensively, sick of his criticism.

'I suppose not, when it's all you have to do all day,' he dismissed harshly.

'It isn't!'

'I'm sure it isn't,' he derided with a humourless smile. 'Now let's get this over with,' he added decisively. 'I'll throw in a necklace to match the bracelet, arrange for you to stay at a hotel until you can find—somewhere else to live,' his mouth twisted. 'As long as you move out tomorrow and don't bother Matt again.'

'And if I don't?' she challenged.

His mouth thinned. 'As I said, I could make things very unpleasant for you.'

She smiled, confident that this man could do nothing to hurt her. 'You're going to feel extremely foolish when you realise what a mistake you've made,' she assured him.

His eyes narrowed. 'You're staying in Matt's apartment, there's no mistake about that.'

Charly could sense he was becoming uneasy about her cool control, her smile widening. 'No, there's no mistake about that,' she agreed.

'And that story about the fire is pure fiction,' he accused.

'Is it?'

'Oh to hell with this!' he moved restlessly. 'The jewellery will be delivered to you here tomorrow morning, make sure you leave then.'

'Don't you think you should talk to Matt before doing this?' she reasoned.

'No, I don't!' He slammed out of the apartment.

Charly's breath was expelled in a tense sigh, shaking her head to suddenly look down at her watch; she was going to be over an hour late for her dinner date.

But she couldn't help wondering, as she drove to the restaurant, what Aaron Grantley's reaction was going to be once he had spoken to Matt tomorrow.

CHAPTER TWO

THE office building of Hartall Industries was one of the most attractive and luxurious in London. Charly's father had always maintained that to be someone you had to *look* like someone. Fortunately his business partner had agreed with him, and from simply looking like someone the two men had *become* someone.

She greeted most of the employees by name as she made her way across the reception, to the private lift, and up to the top floor. Another of her father's sayings, when you *were* someone, it was pure stupidity to forget the people who helped you *stay* someone. He had been on a first-name basis with everyone who worked for him, from the errand boy to his highest executive. Charly couldn't boast the same yet, but she had only been in charge just over a year, and most of that time had been spent learning how to be the Chairwoman of Hartall Industries.

'Get Ian Anderson for me, please, Sarah,' she instructed her secretary on the way through to her own office, feeling at ease among the comfortable opulence of the solid oak desk, cream leather suite, dark brown carpet, several of her favourite paintings on the walls. She had made several small changes since she took over, but not many, having helped with the original design of the office.

Rocharlle Allenby-Hart. Was she really the

'rich bitch' Aaron Grantley had accused her of being? It was true that her parents were already very rich by the time she was born, and she, a late addition to their lives, had wanted for nothing. It was also true that James had been extremely rich when she married him. But whoever had quipped 'money can't buy you happiness' had known what he was talking about! She was richer now than her parents or James had ever been, had made even more of a success of the company since she took over, but her parents were gone, and so was James. And she certainly wasn't happy.

She picked up the receiver on the second ring, having been lost in thought as she stared out of the window. 'Yes, Sarah?' she prompted briskly.

'Mr Anderson is on line one,' her secretary informed her lightly.

For a moment she had forgotten her request for Sarah to call him. 'Put him through,' she instructed softly.

'Charly, how lovely to hear from you.' The man who had been her father's lawyer before hers, greeted her cheerfully. 'I was going to call you myself later.'

'Ian,' she returned abruptly, able to visualise the senior partner of Anderson, Anderson, and McCloed in his book-lined office, the decor comfortable to say the least, not at all musty and dusty the way most people imagined a lawyer's office to be. Ian was another advocate of her father's rule, his offices were the epitome of elegance and comfort. 'I'm not sure you'll still be pleased to hear from me at the end of this conversation,' she added ruefully.

'Oh?' he prompted guardedly.

Charly smiled; Ian had a lawyer's usual reserve, despite knowing her for years. And this time perhaps he had reason to have; she was very displeased about the turn her negotiations for Shevton House had taken. 'Aaron Grantley knows the identity of his competitor in the Shevton House deal,' she came straight to the point.

'Are you sure?' The frown could be heard in his tone of voice.

'I spoke to the man myself yesterday,' she revealed with a sigh. 'Or rather, *he* spoke to me,' she amended ruefully, remembering the conversation—vividly. No one had ever made the assumption before—erroneous or otherwise—that she was any man's mistress, not even James'. 'He left me in no doubt that he was well aware I was the other party interested in the deal. I told you I wanted my involvement kept strictly private,' she reminded hardly, having been completely shaken the evening before when Aaron Grantley had so casually mentioned her interest in a deal she had considered not to be public knowledge. Years of hiding her true feelings had enabled her to hide her shock, but nevertheless it had greatly disturbed her.

'I've done exactly as you instructed, Charly,' Ian sounded concerned. 'You don't suppose Shevton himself would have——'

'He would have if he knew I was behind the second offer he received—did he?'

'Well, I may have mentioned——'

'Ian, I told you not to reveal my identity,' she cut in angrily.

'I know,' he soothed. 'But the man was proving

difficult, and I thought he would keep the information to himself. He wanted to make sure the house that's been in his family for centuries wasn't going to be knocked down and the estate built on. I had to tell him who you were to convince him you didn't have anything like that in mind, that's why I was going to call you later. I had no idea Grantley would actually confront you with the offer. I also have to tell you Shevton leans more towards you, he doesn't particularly want the place to be turned into a hotel.'

'You told him my plans for the house?' she demanded sharply.

'Of course not,' Ian denied. 'But he knows the way you do business.'

Charly sighed. 'He now also knows who the two bidders are and can play one off against the other.'

'I had to stall him in a hurry,' Ian defended. 'Otherwise he would have let the deal go directly to Grantley; he wasn't much in favour of letting it go to an anonymous party for mysterious reasons.'

'Very well, Ian, I can see you didn't have any choice,' she accepted heavily. 'But I'm not happy about the situation.'

'I can understand that,' he acknowledged ruefully. 'But I knew this was one deal you wouldn't want to lose, and I couldn't contact you last night when I called your apartment.'

'I've been staying at a friend's,' she explained in a preoccupied voice.

'I'm really sorry about all this, I had no idea Shevton would tell Grantley who you were.'

'It's done now,' she dismissed abruptly. 'Keep

me informed on your progress—or lack of it,' she added flatly, knowing they were in for a long haul.

'I will. And, Charly, I really am sorry,' he sighed.

'No harm done,' she assured him with more confidence than she felt. Richard Shevton would have had to have been told of her identity eventually, she knew that, just as she couldn't dictate what he did with that information. He must be more of a businessman than she had realised, she decided. The congenial owner of Shevton House and its surrounding thousand acres didn't come over as being shrewd when it came to business, but Charly knew better than anyone how deceptive appearances could be.

'Sarah.' She looked up with a smile as her secretary came in answer to her call. 'I have a feeling a Mr Aaron Grantley will either be telephoning or coming here in person some time today; I want you to make sure he knows I'm unavailable,' she frowned. She had no doubt that when Matt told the other man *she* was Rocharlle Hart he would demand an explanation from her. She would have given him one last night if he had given her the opportunity to do so. Now she didn't feel that she owed him anything, after all he was the one who had jumped to conclusions.

'Yes, Mrs Hart,' Sarah looked puzzled by the request.

Charly gave a rueful smile. 'He's been making a nuisance of himself.' That wasn't exactly a lie, he was a nuisance, and she also knew Sarah would be even more determined to keep Aaron Grantley at bay if she thought he was one of the numerous men who believed it would be nice to marry her money. She had met a lot of them the last year.

'I'll make sure he doesn't bother you,' Sarah told her firmly.

She didn't normally need help to deter the sort of man she had implied Aaron Grantley to be, had been brought up as Rocharlle Allenby, had cut her adult teeth on fortune-hunters. One of the pluses in becoming James's wife was that he had been even richer than she. But of course he had wanted something from her far more important to him than money, and marrying her had instantly given him that.

By late afternoon she had begun to think she had been wrong about Aaron Grantley's next move; there had been no contact from him. Then just after four she heard raised voices in the outer office. Aaron Grantley didn't sound as if he were accepting Sarah's claim that she wasn't available. Charly thought of going to the younger woman's rescue, but that would only make a liar out of Sarah. It would also make *her* look ridiculous. She realised now she should never have given Sarah that instruction, should have known Aaron Grantley wasn't the sort of man to be fobbed off with such an excuse.

She stood up slowly as her office door was flung open, the man himself standing there, very dark and attractive in an iron-grey pin-striped suit. His eyes narrowed on her, and Charly tried to see herself as he must see her, the long golden hair confined in a neat pleat at the back of her head, the black business suit and white blouse with its bow-neckline smart rather than feminine.

She looked completely different from the woman he had met the previous evening.

'I'm sorry, Mrs Hart.' Sarah glared at Aaron Grantley. 'He just pushed past me,' she muttered indignantly.

'It's all right, Sarah,' she soothed. 'I'll deal with Mr Grantley myself,' she added hardly.

The green eyes glittered vengefully. 'I know we argued last night, sweetheart,' he murmured huskily, crossing the room to her side, 'but I don't think that's any reason to be so formal.' He put his arm about her waist to pull her close to the hardness of his body. 'After all, we are engaged to be married,' he said challengingly, his head bending down to hers.

Charly only had tome to register Sarah's gasp of surprise before coolly firm lips claimed hers, his arms about her, one of his hands pressed to the back of her head, preventing her moving away. He kissed her with deliberate thoroughness, savouring the taste of her lips, the probing of his tongue only withdrawn as Charly's small white teeth bit down sharply on the tender flesh.

'Vixen!' he grated before turning to Sarah with a totally charming smile. 'A lovers' quarrel,' he drawled.

Sarah looked totally disconcerted, and Charly couldn't blame her!

'Mr Grantley——'

'Sweetheart, do stop calling me that.' His eyes promised retribution if she didn't! 'And do let this young lady leave so that we don't embarrass her any further with our disagreement.'

Charly gave him a furious look before turning

to her secretary. 'Thank you, Sarah.' She gave a rueful smile. 'I can handle this now.'

'Can you?' Aaron Grantley challenged softly after Sarah had left them, the younger woman still frowning her confusion.

'Yes,' she snapped, moving pointedly away from him. 'I gather you've spoken to Matt.'

'Graphically,' he drawled.

'I'm sure,' her mouth twisted. 'So now you know I'm the "rich bitch" who is trying to ruin your bid for Shevton House.'

He grinned, looking about the room appreciatively 'Mrs Hart apparently likes to surround herself with luxury,' he derided.

'Mrs Hart *earned* this luxury,' she told him tightly, taking the bronze sculpture of a horse out of his hand and placing it back on her desk-top.

'That isn't what I heard,' he mocked, stretching his long length out in one of the armchairs, watching her through narrowed lids. 'You took over when your husband died. Which brings me to the point of why you lied about your name yesterday,' he added sharply.

'I didn't lie.' Her eyes flashed silver. 'My name is Allenby.'

'Was,' Aaron Grantley corrected abruptly. 'Before you married the son of your father's business partner seven years ago. Maybe you did *earn* this company after all,' he derided. 'The marriage was certainly a convenient one.' He raised mocking brows.

'I don't have to explain myself to you——'

'I doubt Rocharlle Hart ever explains herself to anyone. How did you ever get a name like Rocharlle, anyway?' he taunted.

'My parents.'

'That's obvious,' he dismissed mockingly. 'But it isn't what I meant.'

'Rowena and Charles,' she explained impatiently. 'When they were told I was to be an only child they named me after both of them.'

'It would have been easier to call you Charlotte after your father,' Aaron Grantley derided.

It would have been a lot less embarrassing too; her unusual first name had been a talking point all her life. 'You didn't come here to talk about my name——'

'In part I did,' his voice hardened. 'Why didn't you tell me last night who you were?'

'For the same reason you came here today and acted as if our engagement were a reality; which incidentally I want you to correct before you leave—I was angry,' she bit out. 'Matt innocently told you I was staying at his apartment, and then because you were told it was a woman and not a man as you had supposed you assumed I had to be his mistress.'

He shrugged broad shoulders, perfectly relaxed. 'I'm still not sure that isn't true.'

Charly gasped. 'I thought you said you had spoken to Matt?'

'I have,' he nodded. 'But like you, he doesn't feel he has to explain himself. He's mad as hell at both Molly and me for jumping to conclusions,' he added ruefully.

'He's told Molly the truth?'

'Not exactly,' Aaron Grantley derided. 'Apparently she's a little emotional at the moment, and he seems to think we've complicated the situation by pretending to be engaged, believes that if he told her the truth now Molly would think he had something to hide.'

Charly sighed. 'I'm inclined to agree with him.'

'I'm willing to accept that,' Aaron Grantley nodded. 'Although Molly's emotional state seems a little convenient to me.'

She gave him a disparaging look. 'Are you always this suspicious?'

'Only when I find a beautiful woman staying at my best friend's apartment,' he drawled.

'I hope to be moving out at the end of the week,' Charly snapped.

'To go where?'

'My own home, of course,' she told him impatiently.

'Ah yes, the one that's been damaged by fire.'

'Mr Grantley, I don't care for your tone——'

'And I don't care for this whole charade,' he rasped, his eyes bright with anger. 'Especially now that I know the woman I'm engaged to is also the woman who's interfering in my property deal.'

'There are some that would say you have that the wrong way around, Mr Grantley,' she returned coldly.

'Aaron,' he instructed tensely. 'Shevton was on the point of accepting my offer when you came along with a better one,' he scowled.

'And you counter-offered.'

'And so did you,' he ground out. 'How high are you prepared to go?'

'I don't believe that is any of your business,' she snapped indignantly.

'What the hell does Hartall Industries want

with a house like that and a thousand acres?' His eyes were narrowed.

Hartall Industries didn't want them at all; the offer to buy was a purely personal one. But obviously Aaron Grantley wasn't aware of that, at least.

'I suppose you plan to turn it in to yet another hotel?' she scorned.

His mouth tightened. 'You have to see that it would be ideal.'

'It could have other uses,' she dismissed.

'Don't tell me, as a health-farm for all your over-indulged friends,' he derided. 'Or perhaps as a clinic where they can go to "dry out",' he added contemptuously. 'I hear that's very fashionable nowadays.'

'I don't have any friends that need to "dry out",' Charly snapped at his condescension. 'Just as it's none of your business what I do with Shevton House once I've bought it.'

'*If* you buy it,' he corrected gratingly. 'Which you won't,' he said confidently.

'I wouldn't put money on it,' she warned him softly, her grey gaze calm and confident.

'It's perfect for what I want,' he announced arrogantly. 'The building itself, and its location in that little cove is ideal too. You aren't thinking of going in to the hotel business yourself, are you?' he mocked.

'No,' she dismissed with a derisive laugh. 'I've stayed at several of your hotels in the past, Mr— Aaron, and I don't think I could compete.' His hotels offered the sort of first-class accommodation James had always insisted on when they travelled abroad. 'I'm sure Shevton House would make a very good hotel, I just happen to have other plans for it.'

'Shevton isn't likely to sell to either of us now until he gets top dollar,' Aaron grimaced.

She shrugged. 'We both know it's worth it.'

Green eyes narrowed thoughtfully. 'You must want it very badly.'

'Yes,' she confirmed flatly.

He continued to look at her steadily for several seconds, then he shrugged. 'May the best man—person, win.'

Her mouth twisted. 'Oh, I will,' she assured him.

Aaron looked amused. 'That might be difficult, as I intend Shevton House to be mine.'

'We'll see,' she said enigmatically.

'You weren't in for your delivery this morning, so I brought this with me.' He drew out a jewellery box from his pocket, holding it out to her.

'You must realise now that I don't want—or need—the bracelet and necklace,' she told him stiffly.

'It did occur to me,' he drawled. 'So I took them back and got you this instead.'

Charly took the velvet box uncertainly, flicking open the lid. Inside was a gold charm bracelet, but it was the charms attached to it that made her smile, tiny animals all made in minute detail. 'It's beautiful,' she smiled up at Aaron, frowning as she saw the last charm. 'But what's this?' she held up the miniature engagement and wedding rings, the emerald in the former obviously genuine.

'Obligatory, I'm afraid,' he grimaced. 'Window dressing for Molly tonight.'

Charly looked up at him slowly. 'I thought we had agreed we would make my excuses?'

'Hm,' he sighed. 'I'm afraid, as Matt pointed out to me, it would look a bit odd, to Molly, if we broke off our engagement so quickly. Which is why I also purchased this,' he took a ring-box out of his other pocket.

'Oh no,' Charly put her hands behind her back, staring with horror at the finger-sized replica of the emerald ring on the charm bracelet, the emerald the size of a penny. 'I'm not wearing that,' she shook her head.

'I know we told Molly we weren't bothering with an engagement, but——'

'I am not wearing it.' She repressed a shiver of revulsion as she imagined the gold shackle around her finger. 'I'm allergic to rings,' she told him breathlessly.

'To the gold, you mean?' he frowned.

'No—to wearing them!' This time she couldn't hold back the shudder. 'They're a licence to imprison.'

His brows rose. 'So the marriage wasn't so convenient after all,' he drawled.

She looked at him sharply. 'I don't wish to talk about my marriage.'

'There seems to be quite a few things you refuse to talk about,' Aaron taunted.

'Have I tried to pry into your private life?' Her eyes shone silver. 'Have I asked even one question?'

'You asked if I were married,' he reminded.

She sighed. 'In the circumstances I would have

thought you would be as averse to the thought of my wearing your ring as I am,' she derided.

'But I know it's only temporary.'

'It's also unnecessary. Thank you, but no thank you,' she said firmly. 'And are you absolutely sure you can't get me out of dinner this evening?' she frowned. 'I'd really rather not go.'

'Matt seemed to think it was necessary.' He pocketed the ring-box.

She chewed on her inner lip. 'Very well then—if I have no choice.'

'My ego has taken a severe beating since I met you,' Aaron drawled dryly.

'I don't think it's going to do it much harm,' Charly derided.

'You aren't exactly lacking in self-confidence yourself, you know,' he pointed out softly.

Perhaps if he had met her a year ago he would have thought differently. Six years of marriage to a man as strong-willed as James had stripped her of most of the poise and confidence that had been imbued in to her at the finishing-school she had attended in Switzerland. When a man was as assured and arrogant as James had been something had to give in a marriage, and for the sake of peace it had always been Charly. It would never happen to her again, she was her own woman now, and intended to remain that way.

'I'm Rocharlle Allenby-Hart, remember?' she drawled. 'With the gold spoon in my mouth.'

He looked at her thoughtfully. 'Maybe that gold becomes a little heavy to carry at times,' he murmured.

She wasn't sure if he meant literally or

figuratively—whichever one he was right! 'I can live with it,' she mocked.

'Who couldn't?' he derided. 'And if Matt isn't the man in your life then who is?'

She avoided his probing eyes. 'There isn't one. My husband has only been dead a year,' she defended—and then mentally chastised herself for doing so; she had given up justifying her actions after James died. 'Now if you'll excuse me,' she added briskly, 'I have work to do . . .'

'Buying country houses being part of it,' he mocked.

'Yes,' she acknowledged challengingly.

'We'll see,' Aaron murmured.

She could see the return of challenge in his own eyes, and knew that he was enjoying himself. James had enjoyed challenges too, an easy conquest held no interest for him. But she hadn't known that until it was too late, until she found him in her cousin's arms, Jocelyn treating him in the same casual way James regarded Charly. And how James had loved it. And how he had loved Jocelyn too. But when she had asked him for a divorce he hadn't wanted Jocelyn enough to give up the one thing he did want from his marriage to Charly. And then when he had decided *he* wanted a divorce he had once again used the one threat against her guaranteed to make her agree to anything he wanted.

'Where have you gone to?'

She focused her attention on Aaron Grantley with effort, having forgotten his presence as she thought of that last conversation with James that had ended in tragedy. 'Nowhere, Mr Grantley.'

She moved to sit behind her desk. 'For a moment you reminded me of someone,' she added as he seemed to expect more.

His eyes narrowed. 'They seemed unhappy thoughts.'

'They were,' she acknowledged bluntly.

'I realise we got off to a bad start last night——'

'We didn't get off to a start at all,' she corrected abruptly. 'You threw out a lot of groundless accusations, bullied me into acting like your girlfriend——'

'No one bullied you into anything,' Aaron cut in. 'I don't think anyone ever could—What did you say?' he frowned as she muttered something under her breath.

She straightened her shoulders. 'I said they could try,' she spoke loud enough for him to hear this time.

He shrugged dismissively. 'You wanted to put Molly's mind at rest,' he stated firmly.

'Matt adores her,' she said flatly.

'He wouldn't be the first man in love with his wife to be attracted to another woman,' Aaron spoke hardly.

'What time are we expected for dinner this evening?' she ignored the question in his tone.

'Eight o'clock.'

She nodded. 'I'll drive myself down,' she told him briskly. 'I expect to be working late.'

'I'll call for you.'

'I'd prefer to drive myself,' she said determinedly.

'Independent, huh?' he derided.

'Absolutely.' Cold grey eyes met his amused gaze.

'James Hart must have been a bastard,' he said with narrowed eyes.

'He was a very charming and well-liked man,' she stated flatly.

'But hell to live with, I bet.'

Hell exactly described what it had been like to live with James. 'I was married to him for six years,' she taunted. 'So it can't have been all that bad.'

'Bad enough,' Aaron said dryly. 'You have Matt's home address?'

'Yes.' She met his gaze challengingly, daring him to make something of that fact.

He nodded. 'Try not to be late; it might be awkward trying to explain the non-appearance of my "fiancée".'

As she had been the one to actually announce their engagement to Molly she had to go! 'I'll be there,' she assured him.

'Looking a little more like you know what love is, I hope,' he mocked.

She drew in a ragged breath. 'I believe, of the two of us, I am in a better position to have known the emotion than you are!' she scorned harshly. She certainly knew what love *wasn't*!

'If you mean I've never been in love with a woman then that's true. But I do know what love is; my home life as a child was a very happy one. My parents always showed their love for me and each other.'

'It wasn't so different in my home,' she told him hardly.

'I take it your own child hasn't fared as well,' Aaron drawled.

Charly stiffened, her face paling. 'I don't have

a child,' she said between numbed lips.

He frowned. 'But I thought——'

'Whoever your informant was, Mr Grantley, they are out of date,' Charly looked at him coldly, the trembling of her hands hidden beneath the desk. 'My daughter was in the car with James when he crashed. She died too.'

'I didn't know . . .'

She didn't talk to anyone of the agonisingly slow loss of her daughter, of the hatred she had for James because of that even though he, too, was dead and unable to defend himself. There *was* no defence for what he had done!

'I had no idea,' Aaron Grantley sounded concerned. 'Charly, I——'

'I don't need your sympathy,' she snapped, her mouth tight. 'Sympathy can't bring back Stephanie.'

'Or your husband,' he put in softly.

'I'm sure it must be obvious that I don't want James back,' she rasped.

'I did get that impression, yes,' he confirmed dryly. 'What did the poor guy do to you?'

'He married me, Mr Grantley.' She stood up, her eyes cold.

'I see,' he frowned.

'I doubt it,' she derided. 'Now if you wouldn't mind, I have an appointment in a few minutes . . .' It was a lie, but she didn't want to talk any more just now, this man was getting to the vulnerability of her private grief without even seeming to try.

He shrugged. 'I have to be somewhere else myself,' he nodded. 'But I'll expect to see you tonight, wearing the bracelet as I can't persuade you to wear the ring.'

'Take the ring back where you bought it, Mr Grantley,' she advised dryly. 'And get your money back.'

'You really are allergic, huh?'

'They make me nauseous!'

'You're going to make some lucky man a good mistress one day,' he mused.

Her eyes flashed deeply silver. 'It's only men's delusion that women are subservient to them, *we* know that we actually aren't. Some man might make me a good lover,' she said with distaste, unable to envisage the day that she ever took a lover.

'Don't you think that's taking your independence too far? No, probably not,' he grimaced. 'Not for Rocharlle Allenby-Hart.'

'It doesn't matter who I am,' she dismissed. 'I'm just a woman——'

'A very bitter one,' he put in softly. 'You're too young to let one bad experience sour you.'

'Age has nothing to do with it,' she scorned. 'And it wasn't an experience, Mr Grantley,' she added hardly. 'It was a marriage. At least, I thought it was.'

He looked as if he wanted to say more, then he shrugged dismissively. 'I'll see you tonight.'

Charly was still standing tensely in front of the window when Sarah entered her office a few minutes later. She turned to face the younger woman, her features schooled into their usual calm.

'Are you really going to marry Mr Grantley?' Sarah was too stunned to be politely silent about the man who had just left.

Charly gave a rueful smile. 'Didn't you

recognise a ruse to get in to see me without an appointment?' she said lightly, having decided this was the only way to treat Aaron Grantley's vengeful statement, having no intention of acting a part at work too.

'But——' the other woman looked confused. 'Is that all it was?'

'Of course,' Charly smiled, meeting her secretary's gaze steadily. She would not find herself intimidated by Aaron Grantley in any aspect of her business life!

'Oh.' Sarah looked disappointed.

Charly laughed softly. 'He's much too bossy for me,' she teased.

'But gorgeous, don't you think?' her secretary said eagerly.

She grimaced. 'Very,' she admitted. 'If he calls or turns up like that again perhaps you had better just let him in,' she said dryly. 'I don't think we need a repeat of today's scene.'

Sarah looked disappointed. 'So you really aren't going to marry him?'

She shook her head. 'I'm not going to marry anyone, I'm leaving that to you.' Her secretary was marrying her long-time boyfriend in a couple of months.

Sarah nodded, turning to leave. 'By the way, I like your bracelet. It's new, isn't it?' she teased knowingly.

Charly couldn't prevent the colour that brightened her cheeks. 'Yes, it's new,' she confirmed abruptly, wishing she had never entered into this deceit with Aaron Grantley.

But she knew better than anyone how painful it was to believe your husband had another woman, how the bitterness and uncertainty eroded away at love and finally left only bitterness. She had never met Matt's wife Molly before, but he had spoken of her often, always with deep love, and she hadn't liked to think his kind gesture of letting her use his apartment while her own was being redecorated would result in a serious misunderstanding between him and his wife. Jocelyn had once made her very aware of the fact that her involvement with James wasn't quite so innocent.

At eighteen Charly had suddenly found herself without parents, half owner of the Hartall empire, with not a clue how to cope with the sudden responsibility. James' parents, Will and Glenda, had been on a weekend trip with her own parents to Scotland, their plane going down on the return journey, all four passengers and the crew killed. If it hadn't been for James' support during the next few months she didn't know how she would have got through. Ten years her senior, he had been involved in the running of Hartall Industries for some years, taking over the reins of complete control with no trouble at all.

With the difference in their ages Charly hadn't socially had a lot to do with the son of her father's partner, but during the next few months she came to rely on him totally, for the running of the company and also for her mental salvation, the two of them spending most of their evenings together. When she had begun to fall in love with him she didn't know, but suddenly it was a fact, her contentment complete when James asked her to marry him. Of course he had used words like love and forever in his proposal, what he should have said were gain and convenience! In her youthfully trusting innocence she had entrusted the running of Hartall Industries to James. Ian Anderson had advised her against such a move, but she had laughed off his caution. After all, James was her husband, and she trusted him implicitly.

For two years she had lived in ignorant bliss, had given birth to Stephanie during their first year of marriage, giving almost all her attention to the beautiful baby that was her daughter. When she first heard the rumours of James' mistress she had dismissed them as malicious gossip; she and James were ecstatically happy together. But the rumours persisted, and she finally asked James about it. He had flown into a temper, saying it was her fault, that she gave all her attention to the baby and ignored him and his needs. The fact that he did have another woman was blow enough, that it was her fault affected her badly. She began to put James first in everything, to give her love and attention to Stephanie only when they were alone during the day, virtually ignoring the confused baby when James was at home. That hadn't satisfied him either, he accused her of suffocating him with her love, and within a few weeks there was yet another woman. And then another. And then another . . .

During the following years she lost count of the amount of women that passed briefly through James' life, for the most part ignoring their existence, her confidence in herself completely undermined, leaning more heavily on James than ever in her effort to hold on to their marriage. Stephanie thought her father was wonderful, and by the time she got past the baby stage he was taking quite an interest in her too. Just seeing them together was enough to show Charly that none of the other women really meant anything to James.

On their fifth wedding anniversary they had given a family party, James' absence when it came time for them to receive her uncle's good luck toast causing her to stumble across James in the arms of his latest mistress. She had heard noises from their bedroom, had guessed James must be in there, the smile freezing on her lips as she walked in on the partly undressed couple, James glaring at her furiously, Jocelyn giving a self-satisfied smile. Charly had hastily backed out of the room, too shocked to even speak.

She had returned downstairs to the party as if nothing had happened, too numbed to even think just yet, but knowing she couldn't cause a scene with all these people in the house. James and Jocelyn had rejoined the party several minutes later, her stricken gaze meeting James' bored one as her uncle finally made his toast to them.

She avoided being near either Jocelyn or James the rest of the evening, almost at breaking point by the time they had seen the last guest depart, her tension causing her to tremble uncontrollably.

James poured himself a drink, facing her across the lounge. 'I suppose you want to talk now,' he drawled.

'How could you?' she accused. 'For years I've ignored your affairs, but I won't allow this relationship with Jocelyn to continue.'

Blue eyes glazed over with an icy chill. '*You*

won't allow?' he repeated softly. 'Since when have I asked your permission to do anything?'

He had never spoken to her in quite this contemptuous way before, and Charly could only stare at him, waiting for the next blow to fall. As she knew it must.

'I married you for one reason and one reason only,' he told her in a coldly cruel voice. 'To have complete control over Hartall Industries——'

'James . . .?' she gasped her disbelief.

'Which you so kindly gave me,' he taunted, drinking some of his whisky. 'I've allowed you to stay my wife the last five years, don't force me to choose between you and Jocelyn; you would lose,' he scorned.

Charly dropped down dazedly into one of the armchairs. 'You—You've never loved me?'

'I've never been interested in small, childish blondes,' he dismissed harshly. 'You're satisfying enough in bed but out of it you have the intelligence of a schoolgirl!'

She wanted to point out to him that when they had married she had only recently stopped being a schoolgirl, that instead of growing and maturing in her marriage she had remained youthfully insecure, unsure of her husband and their life together. But once again she remained silent.

'I want Jocelyn in my life,' he told her softly. 'And I'll have her for as long as I want her.'

This time Charly did speak. 'In that case I want a divorce,' she stated flatly.

'No,' he derided.

'You can't stop me——'

'Stephanie . . .?'

Charly paled, looked at him sharply. 'What about her?'

'If you divorce me you will take your half of the company with you,' he bit out hardly. 'And I can't allow that. If you insist on divorce, Charly, I'll fight you for custody of Stephanie.'

'You would lose,' she gasped.

'Would I?' he mocked. 'Whatever else I've been I've also been a good father to Stephanie, not even you can dispute that. I love her. And the courts are more inclined to listen to the wishes of a father nowadays when it comes to giving custody of children.'

'If you love her as you say you do then you won't put her through that.' Charly shook her head.

'Oh, I love her,' he confirmed grimly. 'But I want Hartall Industries more!'

'And Jocelyn,' she said dully.

'And Jocelyn,' he nodded challengingly.

Charly had stood up with all the dignity she possessed. 'Even though there will be no divorce our marriage is still at an end,' she announced coldly, taking the first painful step towards emotional independence, knowing James had never loved her killing what little affection had remained for him from that first heady love. 'I will never again share the bedroom with you that you were in earlier with Jocelyn; I shall be sleeping in the spare room from now on.'

'Please yourself,' he shrugged dismissively. 'It won't be any great loss.'

She was past feeling pain at that moment, but once the numbness of the situation wore off she became sensitive to every cutting and derogatory remark James made. The next year was unbearable, James not even trying to hide his affair with Jocelyn now, often escorting the other woman to parties that would normally be attended by his wife. For Stephanie's sake Charly had borne the humiliation, feeling only relief when James himself had told her he now wanted the divorce, and in return for giving her custody of Stephanie he wanted complete control of Hartall Industries. She had had to refuse, Hartall Industries was Stephanie's inheritance. James had driven off with Stephanie in his car after telling her she would never see her daughter again.

It had been James she had never seen again, Stephanie's injuries in the accident so severe that she lay in a coma for the next two months before finally dying.

That had completed Charly's maturity, and she had promised herself that no man would ever hurt her like that again. She had thrown all her energies into making Hartall Industries more successful than it had ever been, and she had succeeded more than her wildest dreams. She certainly wasn't going to let another arrogantly assured man beat her in what she considered a very important property deal.

She picked up the telephone on her desk. 'Sarah? Get me Ian Anderson,' she instructed curtly.

CHAPTER THREE

SHE enjoyed the lengthy drive to Berkshire, rarely found the time or occasion to get out of London nowadays. She envied Matt his beautiful country home, appreciating why he found it nicer to live here even though it meant, with his duties at the hospital, he occasionally had to stay the night at his apartment in town. Surely knowing he had the secluded house and lovely family to come home to more than made up for that.

She had little difficulty finding the house, parking her Porsche next to the bottle green sports model Jaguar already in the driveway, guessing who that belonged to. The man seemed to have a thing about the colour green. She had to admit that the green of his eyes was—Was what? She wasn't going to fall for a good-looking charmer a second time. She wasn't going to fall for any man!

'Charly!' Matt met her at the door, a tall distinguished looking man, his blond hair showing signs of greying, his eyes a warm brown. 'Oh, love, I can't tell you how sorry I am about this mess.' He helped her off with her coat, handing it to the butler before dismissing him. 'I never dreamt when I offered you the use of the apartment that it would come to this,' he frowned.

'It's all right.' She put her hand comfortingly on his arm. 'I should have realised at the time that it was a bad idea. Once I realised the conclusion Molly had come to I was glad to help. Although maybe I just complicated things even more,' she grimaced.

'I thought so,' he agreed consideringly. 'But not since talking to Molly. She's a little emotional at the moment, this third pregnancy is——'

'You're having another child? How wonderful!' She was genuinely excited for them.

'I think so,' he sighed. 'But Molly feels it's too soon after Tommy; he's only just a year old, you know. In the circumstances I think you and Aaron did the right thing; Molly has enough to cope with at the moment without doubt between us.'

Charly frowned her concern. 'Is there anything I can do to help?'

He put his hand over hers. 'You've already done enough,' he said gratefully. 'Without you——'

'I think your wife is feeling neglected, Matt.' Aaron Grantley told him with forced cheerfulness as he joined them, turning narrowed eyes on Charly. 'Ah, my charming fiancée,' he drawled mockingly.

'Aaron——'

'Charly and I understand each other,' the other man assured him harshly. 'Molly,' he prompted.

To say this man looked devastatingly attractive in an evening suit was an understatement; he looked magnificent, wide shoulders, tapered waist and thighs. His skin looked very tanned against the whiteness of his shirt, his eyes glittering like twin emeralds. It was the anger in his eyes that brought Charly to her senses, challenge in her gaze.

'That was a touching scene I just interrupted,' he drawled insultingly.

'Wasn't it?' she returned sweetly, not prepared to justify her liking for Matt to this man.

'I thought I told you to stay away from him,' Aaron grated.

She shook her head. 'You told Charly Allenby, not Rocharlle Hart.'

'Don't play games with me,' he warned softly.

'Games?' She raised her brows. 'I don't know what you mean, Mr Grantley.'

'You know,' he rasped.

Charly sighed. 'As usual you're mistaken about the situation,' she snapped. 'Molly's pregnant, did you know?'

His gaze became wary. 'They just told me.'

'That's the emotional state Matt told you about; he's frightened she might lose the baby.'

'Which is why he's got himself involved with you, I suppose,' Aaron scorned. 'Try again, Mrs Hart.'

'I don't have to,' she shrugged. 'My conscience is clear, and that's all I care about. You can take your opinion of me and——' She broke off as Aaron roughly pulled her into his arms and began to kiss her. He didn't even try to make it pleasant for her, kissing her contemptuously, his mouth savaging hers.

'Whoops! Sorry,' Molly told them teasingly.

Charly was released as soon as the other woman returned to the lounge, breathing hard. 'You didn't have to be so rough!' She touched her bruised lips, her lipgloss completely gone, her eyes a dark stormy grey.

Aaron shrugged non-committally. 'You were being indiscreet.'

'I was telling you exactly what I think of you,' she corrected, marching over to the hall mirror to check her appearance; she looked a mess. Her hair had escaped in loose tendrils from the neat pleat at the back of her head, her cheeks were flushed, and her mouth was pink and moist from his rough handling. The silky sheath of her black dress still looked as good, but she definitely needed tidying. She opened her bag to find her brush.

'Don't bother.' Aaron took hold of her arm to drag her towards the lounge. 'You look as if you've just been kissed.'

'I feel as if I've been savaged!' she glared at him.

'I'm sorry about that,' he sighed. 'But I heard Molly coming, and you didn't exactly sound loverlike,' he derided.

'I sounded angry—which I am,' she snapped. 'I wouldn't do to Molly what you're accusing me of doing; I like her.'

'She likes you too,' he nodded grimly. 'But that's only because she doesn't really know you.'

Charly stiffened. 'Other women's husbands hold no attraction for me.'

He shrugged. 'Maybe Matt forgot to mention he was married until it was too late.'

Her fingers curled about her handbag, only just resisting the impulse to swing her arm and smack him around the face with it. 'Your erroneous opinion of Matt is only superceded by your opinion of me!'

Aaron's mouth twisted. 'Let's just say I'm beginning to realise what your attraction could

be,' he drawled, his gaze lingering appreciatively
on the creamy softness of her breasts exposed by
the low neckline of her dress.

She gave him a look of intense dislike. 'Remarks
like that only emphasize your *lack* of attraction!'

His mouth quirked, the green eyes warm with
enjoyment of this encounter. 'I bet you're a hell-
cat in bed.'

She gasped her outrage at this casually made
statement. 'You'll never know that!' she bit out
angrily.

'I wouldn't be too sure of that,' he mocked.
'You're beginning to interest me.'

Her eyes flashed, her body stiff with indignation. 'And I couldn't be *less* interested in you!'

'I have been known to change a woman's
mind,' he taunted.

'Not mine.' Charly shook her head. 'Now shall
we join Matt and Molly?'

She was aware of him behind her as they
entered the lounge, a little startled when his arm
came possessively about her waist, although the
smile remained on her lips. 'I hope we haven't
kept you waiting,' she greeted smoothly.

'Not at all.' The other woman looked very
attractive in a midnight blue dress, although
Charly doubted the slender style would fit her for
much longer. 'Dinner is only just ready.'

'Congratulations,' Charly told her warmly.
'Matt told me your good news.'

Molly gave a rueful smile. 'I only found out for
certain myself today. In fact, that was why I
needed that old address book from the apartment,'
she explained awkwardly. 'I needed the number
of my gynaecologist.'

'If I'd realised we were celebrating tonight I would have brought champagne,' Aaron said regretfully.

'I'm not allowed to drink alcohol now anyway,' Molly grimaced. 'Even the small glass I am allowed when I'm pregnant makes me sick.'

The pregnancy had obviously come as something of a shock to Molly, it was there in her voice, and Charly was more relieved than ever that she had helped put this woman's mind at rest about Matt and herself. Her own pregnancy seven years ago had been a surprise too, and at nineteen she had found it difficult to cope with the changes in her body. Molly had obviously been through those changes twice before, but as she had probably only just regained her figure after giving birth to one-year-old Tommy she must feel a little anger mixed in with her excitement about the thought of being pregnant again. In the circumstances it was understandable.

'Never mind, love,' Aaron sympathised. 'You only have seven months to go.'

Charly could see it had been the wrong thing to say even as Molly's eyes took on a hunted look.

'I can't cope with it,' Molly suddenly cried. 'It's too much!' She turned and ran from the room.

Charly turned on Aaron. 'You have the sensitivity of a moron!' she snapped, throwing her handbag down in a chair at go after Molly.

'What did I say?' He looked dazed by the scene such a casual remark seemed to have made.

Matt shrugged. 'Pregnancy tends to make a

woman act a bit strange,' he grimaced. 'It's all those hormones going haywire!'

Charly whirled back to face them. 'While the two of you are standing here musing over the quaint little ways of women when they're pregnant perhaps you would like to consider the fact that although seven months may not sound very long to you it is in fact over *half a year!*' She glared at them as she now held their attention. 'You both have your pleasure for half an hour or so, but it's the woman who for the next nine months feels sick, tired, blows up like a balloon, is kicked under the ribcage whenever she tries to get any rest, and on top of all that she has to cope with teasing idiots like you two!' She was breathing hard in her agitation. 'If men were the ones who had to go through all that the birthrate would go down to a dangerous low!'

'When you put it like that . . .' Aaron mocked.

'I do,' she snapped. 'Now I am going to try and calm Molly, I would advise the two of you to try and straighten up your act while I'm gone. You *are* some sort of comedy team, aren't you?' she derided hardly.

'Vicious,' Aaron murmured admiringly.

'I never knew you had a temper, Charly,' Matt said in awe.

Green eyes mocked Charly. 'I have a feeling there's quite a lot you don't know about her, Matt,' he drawled.

Grey clashed with green. 'There's quite a lot you both don't know about me,' she bit out before leaving the room.

She found the other woman upstairs in her

bedroom, deep sobs wracking her body as she lay across her bed.

'I'm sorry,' she choked as she saw Charly, trying to mop up the tears with a tissue. 'You must think I'm awful reacting this way.'

'Not at all,' she assured her softly, sitting on the side of the bed to hand Molly another tissue. 'It isn't easy being pregnant.'

Molly sniffed, the tears ceasing. 'Do you have children? Matt told me you've been married before.'

'No,' she answered regretfully. 'My daughter died——'

'Oh I'm so sorry,' Molly was instantly contrite. 'You must think from the way I've been acting, that I don't want this baby. It isn't that——'

'You just haven't had time to get over your son's birth yet,' she acknowledged ruefully. 'It's supposed to get easier, but I'm not sure it does,' she smiled.

'Tommy wasn't a good baby,' Molly grimaced, sitting up. 'He used to cry a lot, and he didn't really have much of an interest in food. And he's only just started going through the night. Matt's been marvellous——'

'But?' Charly prompted indulgently.

'But he's a doctor,' Molly sighed. 'He's used to going into a ward, seeing his patient, issuing instructions, and then expecting them to be carried out while he goes on to see another patient.'

'And he did the same with you and Tommy,' she said knowingly.

'Sometimes,' Molly nodded. 'It isn't that I

don't want the baby, I just—I'm not sure I can cope with another one just now.'

'Are you sure it isn't just that you're tired?' Charly suggested gently. 'It's hard work bringing up children.'

'Lucy should almost be at school by the time this one is born,' the other woman said heavily. 'But she's so independent anyway, two children both under two is a different matter altogether.'

'It could be fun,' Charly smiled. 'I'm not saying it will be easy, but they should amuse each other to a certain extent, and once the new baby gets over the very young stage it can go on the floor and play with Tommy. I'm sure that at the moment you seem to be constantly telling Lucy she isn't big enough to pick Tommy up?'

'Why . . . yes,' Molly nodded slowly.

'Tommy and the new baby would soon be more or less the same size so you wouldn't have that problem with them. I'm sure it will be hard work, but it could also have its compensations,' she encouraged.

Molly gave a shaky smile. 'You could be right,' she gave a wan smile. 'Matt and Aaron are going to think I'm so stupid,' she grimaced, standing up to repair her make-up. 'Especially for a doctor's wife!'

'I don't think so.' She smiled as she remembered the two men's faces as she left the lounge. 'Not after what I said to them.'

Molly gave her a questioning look. 'What did you say to them?'

'Enough to make them think a little harder next time before speaking,' she mocked.

Molly tidied her hair. 'I'm so happy for you and Aaron; you seem so happy together.'

Her mouth tightened. 'Yes.'

'I—I have a confession to make.' The other woman turned to her. 'Last night, when I came to the apartment, it wasn't just for the address book, I—I thought you were Matt's girlfriend,' she admitted in a self-conscious rush.

Charly kept her expression bland with effort. 'But Matt's married,' she frowned.

'Yes, but I—I knew you were staying at the apartment, and I—I thought——'

'That Matt and I were lovers,' she laughed dismissively, the other woman's admission totally unexpected and taking her slightly off-guard. 'I can't see Aaron liking that, can you?' she teased.

Molly grimaced. 'I have to admit, I didn't like the idea much either!'

'I'm sure you didn't,' she laughed softly. 'Now shall we rejoin the men before they start dinner without us? I don't suppose——'

'Oh, what a beautiful bracelet!' Molly exclaimed, looking at the charm bracelet Charly wore. 'Oh it's lovely,' she admired as she looked at it closely. 'And I see Aaron did buy you a ring after all,' she teased as she saw the two gold ring charms.

'Yes,' Charly answered abruptly.

'I'm so glad he's going to marry you, Charly,' Molly looked at her warmly. 'I'm sure we're going to be good friends.'

'I'm sure we are too,' she agreed with genuine warmth, glad the other woman had been diverted from the subject of the bracelet. She almost hadn't worn it, despite—or *in* spite?—of Aaron's request, but at the last moment decided it was a nice touch.

'Would you like to look in on the children with me?' Molly asked shyly. 'That is, if you——'

'I love children,' Charly assured her, guessing that Stephanie's death was the reason for Molly's sudden hesitation. 'And I'd like to see Lucy and Tommy.'

The little girl was exactly like her mother, dark-haired and pretty, while Tommy was most like Matt, his blond hair in curls, his face still chubby with baby fat, his lashes fanned out across his baby cheeks as he lay asleep in his cot.

'They're adorable,' Charly told the other woman softly as they went downstairs together.

'Yes, they are,' Molly agreed ruefully. 'I feel better about this baby already.'

'I'm glad to hear it, darling,' Matt put his arm about his wife's shoulders as they entered the lounge. 'I was worried about you,' he admitted softly.

'I was being silly,' she snuggled against him. 'Just think, Tommy will have a playmate now.'

Matt looked over his wife's head and gave Charly a grateful smile. 'And Lucy can mother both of them,' he agreed indulgently.

Charly walked at Aaron's side as they went through to the adjoining room to have dinner, studiously avoiding his gaze.

'That was very nice of you,' he murmured so that only she could hear.

'I can be nice when I like the person involved,' she returned huskily, not looking at him.

He chuckled appreciatively. 'God, I bet you're dynamite in bed!'

She turned to him furiously. 'Keep your opinions to yourself!' she snapped.

He shook his head mockingly. 'All that energy wasted on just talking!'

'How would you like to sit down to dinner without your "fiancée"?' she threatened.

'You won't leave.'

'Try me.'

Aaron sighed. 'I was only making conversation.'

'You were being personal!'

'I'm your fiancé——'

Now she did turn to look at him. 'Don't let this bogus engagement make you think you have any rights over me,' she warned harshly. 'Physically, or in any other way. Because if you push me too far I won't hesitate to let you go through this alone.'

'You wouldn't do that,' he claimed confidently. 'You wouldn't hurt Molly in that way.'

No, she couldn't do it, especially now that Molly had admitted believing Matt to be Charly's lover. But the look she gave Aaron Grantley wasn't in the least defeated. 'I'm Rocharlle Hart, remember, "without wants or needs, with only a quest for power". You think someone like that would care who got hurt if events didn't suit me?' she challenged.

He looked at her steadily. 'I think *you* would,' he said slowly.

Her mouth twisted. 'You won't know until you push me too far—and I really wouldn't advise it.'

His look was admiring. 'You've acquired quite a business reputation since you took over from your husband last year; I can see why.'

'Thank you,' she accepted it as the compliment it was, sitting down as he held out her chair for her.

'Matt and I had a talk while you ladies were upstairs,' he spoke loud enough for the other couple to hear too now.

Charly was suddenly wary, not liking the gleam of satisfaction in his eyes. 'Yes?'

'He and Molly haven't been able to get away since Tommy was born, and now that Molly's expecting number three I suggested maybe they would like to go away together for a few days,' he still spoke lightly.

'It sounds like a good idea.' But she still frowned, watching him warily.

'Alone,' he added with slow emphasis, holding her gaze challengingly.

'Yes?' she prompted again, still not sure what point he was trying to make.

'It sounds wonderful, Aaron,' Molly put in lightly. 'But there's only my parents to take care of the children, and while I don't mind leaving the children with them for a day or evening I really feel a few days would be too much for them. They aren't getting any younger, and Tommy is a bit of a handful. It was a nice idea, though,' she sighed at the lost opportunity.

'I wasn't suggesting your parents have the children, Molly.' Aaron still looked at Charly. 'I thought Charly and I could come here and take care of them for you. After all, they know me, and they would soon get used to Charly.'

Molly turned uncertainly to Charly. 'You really wouldn't mind?'

Bastard, Charly's furious gaze transmitted the message to Aaron, knowing he had received the message as his mouth quirked triumphantly. 'No, of course not,' she assured the other woman, avoiding Aaron Grantley's gaze now. 'I'm sure Aaron is excellent at changing nappies,' she added vengefully.

Matt gave a scornful laugh. 'He doesn't know one end of a baby from the other!'

Aaron scowled at him. 'I know a damn sight more than you did when Lucy was born!'

'Not much more,' Molly laughed. 'I sincerely hope you won't let him loose on Tommy, Charly.'

'I think it would be a good idea.' Charly ate her soup with an air of feigned innocence, once again ignoring Aaron's furious gaze. 'It will be good practise for him for when he becomes a father. I'll supervise them to make sure he doesn't do anything drastic with Tommy, Molly, but I do think he should have complete charge of the baby that weekend.' She looked at him challengingly.

His mouth was tight. 'It isn't very likely I'll ever have to take care of a baby.'

'Oh but there might be occasions when you will, Aaron,' Molly put in seriously. 'Matt tells me Charly is an important lady in the world of business; you would have to take your turn in taking care of the children.'

He scowled. 'I'd hire a nanny.'

Charly shook her head. 'I don't believe in them.'

'Then we won't have any children,' he glared.

'I had a feeling that might be your answer,' she said triumphantly, sipping at her wine.

He gave her an impatient look. 'Are we looking after the children next weekend or not?'

'We are,' she nodded, her mouth curved into a smile. 'With an emphasis on the "we".'

'I think we could have an enjoyable break just watching Aaron trying to cope with Tommy,' Matt mocked. 'In a boardroom he's lethal, but he might not have the same success in a nursery.'

'Tommy likes me,' he claimed indignantly.

'You're his favourite uncle,' Matt nodded. 'But he *dislikes* going to bed at night.'

'All kids dislike that,' Aaron shrugged it off as being unimportant.

'But Tommy *really* dislikes it,' his friend taunted. 'To the point where——'

'Don't tell him any more,' Molly pleaded. 'Or he might change his mind about the offer.'

'He won't,' Charly put in firmly. 'Is next weekend okay for you?' she asked the other couple.

A situation Aaron had created to put her at a disadvantage had been neatly turned on him, and she couldn't help feeling satisfied that she had managed to do so. He had been enjoying himself at her expense; she found it infinitely enjoyable that the roles had been reversed!

'Are you really sure you don't mind?' Molly still hesitated about accepting their offer.

'Not at all,' Charly answered smoothly. 'This is a beautiful house, the children look adorable; I'm sure I'll enjoy myself.' The look she shot Aaron told him it would be mainly at his expense.

He turned to Molly. 'We'll only be needing the one bedroom,' he told her. 'Unless you think it would be better for the children if we slept apart?'

The colour came and went in Charly's cheeks in rapid succession, her mouth tight. Aaron had certainly wreaked his vengeance with interest!

'Of course not,' Molly dismissed. 'They're both too young to ask questions.'

'Oh good,' he smiled his satisfaction. 'We haven't liked to be together at the apartment because it seemed as if we were taking advantage of you.'

'We don't mind if Aaron moves in, do we, darling?' Molly shook her head.

Matt looked at Aaron with narrowed eyes. 'I think that's for Charly to say,' he said tightly.

She cleared her throat awkwardly. 'I'm sure Aaron and I can come to some sort of agreement,' she nodded. 'Thank you,' she added abruptly.

Aaron looked at her with amused green eyes. For every verbal and mental battle that she managed to win over this man he paid her back two-fold! That bit about them sharing a bedroom here next weekend had stunned her, the idea of him moving into the apartment with her was unthinkable.

'Don't let Aaron get to you,' Matt advised as she prepared to leave later that evening, Aaron and Molly still in the lounge. 'He's enjoying himself, that's all.'

'Don't worry,' she assured him. 'He doesn't bother me at all.'

'I can try to put off next weekend if you would like me to?' he frowned.

'I wouldn't hear of it.' She shook her head firmly. 'Please don't worry about Aaron, I can handle him.'

'I'll make sure there are two bedrooms ready for you.' Matt said grimly.

'Even if there were only the one we wouldn't

be sharing it,' she told him hardly. 'Aaron would be sleeping on the sofa in the lounge.'

'He can be very persuasive.'

'I'm not interested,' she dismissed.

Matt frowned at the determination in her voice. 'Most women find him very attractive.'

'I'm not denying his attraction, just stating that he doesn't appeal to me.'

'Sure?'

'Very!'

He shrugged wide shoulders. 'As long as this situation isn't bothering you?'

'It isn't.' She shook her head. 'Look, I'm going down to the house tomorrow, why don't you come with me?' she suggested eagerly. 'I'd really like you to see it, to know your opinion of it before I buy it.'

'Charly, I told you——'

'I know,' she soothed. 'And I understand how you feel, but it's something I want to do.'

'I can't let you——'

'It isn't a question of letting me do anything, Matt.' She put her hand on his arm. 'It's something I really need to do.'

He nodded. 'When do you intend going to the house?'

'In the afternoon,' she told him. 'Please come with me,' she encouraged.

'I'll see if I can get away,' he nodded slowly. 'Although I'm not promising anything,' he warned.

'It's enough that you'll try.' Her eyes glowed. 'I'm sure you'll find it's completely suitable.'

'It's convenient anyway,' he grimaced. 'Only a short drive from here.'

'That's one of the reasons I liked it,' she

nodded. 'This way you could still have the best of both worlds.'

'It's time we were going, Charly.' Aaron cut in with rasping tension, Molly behind him.

Charly looked at him steadily. 'I've been waiting for you,' she told him calmly.

His hard green eyes questioned the validity of that fact before he turned to kiss Molly on the cheek. 'Thank you for a lovely evening,' he smiled affectionately. 'If I were you I would make this husband of yours take you shopping for some new clothes for your weekend away.' He looked challengingly at Charly after this last statement, and she frowned her puzzlement. 'Tomorrow,' he added pointedly.

He had overheard part of her conversation with Matt! And from his manner now she could only presume he had come to his own conclusions. She smiled ruefully, her head going back proudly as Aaron's eyes hardened angrily.

'Matt doesn't like to go shopping,' Molly dismissed with a laugh.

'Then perhaps Charly would like to go with you,' he suggested harshly.

'I can't tomorrow, I'm afraid,' she refused softly. 'But I'd love to go with you some other day,' she agreed.

'I'll call you,' Molly nodded eagerly.

'How can you do it?' Aaron demanded impatiently once they were out on the driveway.

'Do what?' She looked up at him innocently.

He glanced over to where Matt and Molly stood together near the front door waiting to wave their goodbyes. 'We can't talk here,' he muttered. 'I'll meet you at the apartment.'

'I'd rather you didn't.'

'Why, is Matt going to suddenly discover there's an emergency at the hospital?' he derided harshly.

'No!' She looked at him defiantly.

His eyes glittered in the darkness. 'Then I'm not asking you if I can come to the apartment; I'm telling you!'

She shrugged. 'In that case I suppose I'll see you later.' She came to an abrupt halt as he grabbed her arm. 'What is it?' she asked impatiently.

'We ought to say good night in the appropriate manner,' he told her roughly.

'It isn't good night,' she pointed out calmly, not at all cowed by his manner.

'Nevertheless, we do have an audience,' he ground out, bending his head to claim her mouth.

But instead of the anger she had been expecting she found only deep sensuality in Aaron's kiss, the slow drugging exploration of her mouth affecting her in spite of herself, her hands about his waist as he curved her body up into his, Charly made aware of every hard plane of his thighs and chest.

Aaron raised his head, his eyes narrowed. 'You're very responsive,' he accused.

She was glad of the darkness to cover her blushes. 'We have an audience, remember,' she said sharply.

He gave her a scornful look. 'Are you hoping to make Matt jealous?' he rasped softly.

She pulled away from him, her gaze contemptuous. 'He's well aware of the fact that I despise you, Mr Grantley,' she dismissed harshly. 'Just as he's aware that your kisses are forced on me.'

His mouth tightened. 'I'll see you back at the apartment.' He turned on his heel and got into the Jaguar, accelerating out of the driveway with a brief wave of his hand to Matt and Molly.

Charly took a little longer to get into her own car, slightly dazed by her reaction to a man she had just claimed to despise.

'Is everything all right?' Matt had joined her beside her car without her being aware of it.

'Yes, of course.' She shook off her feeling of unease, smiling brightly. ''Night, Molly,' she called out to the other woman. 'Good night, Matt,' she turned back to him reassuringly. 'And please don't worry about me.'

'We can end this any time you want to, you know.' He frowned his concern.

'I told you, I can handle the situation and Mr Aaron Grantley!'

But as she drove home she couldn't help wondering if Aaron Grantley weren't more than a match for her, both physically and mentally.

She wasn't in the least surprised when she reached the apartment first, more familiar with the roads than Aaron was likely to be, living in America as he did most of the time. Consequently she was in the lounge enjoying a relaxing drink when the doorbell rang, bracing her shoulders determinedly as she went to answer it.

'I stopped off for some cigarettes,' Aaron explained his lateness as he walked past her into the apartment.

'Please do come in,' she told him with sarcasm as she followed him through to the lounge. 'And

I thought I had made it clear that I don't like anyone smoking near me,' she reminded hardly as he flicked on a gold lighter beneath the cigarette in his mouth, smoke instantly filling the room.

'I need a cigarette,' he rasped unrelentingly.

Charly could feel herself begin to pale as the consequences of someone else 'needing a cigarette' began to wash over her, reliving the nightmare of being dragged through her smoke-filled apartment. 'Would it help if I said please,' she asked faintly.

Puzzlement flickered in deep green eyes before it was quickly replaced with impatience. 'No.'

She moved to the windows, opening one wide despite the cold night air that instantly blew into the room.

'Don't carry this charade into the farcical,' Aaron advised hardly. 'You're just making yourself look ridiculous.'

Anger flared in the depths of silver-grey eyes as she turned back to face him. 'I'd like to show you something that's really ridiculous!' she bit out furiously, marching over to the door and throwing it open. 'Well don't just stand there.' She turned on him. 'Come and see something *really* ridiculous!'

'Charly——'

'What's the matter, Aaron?' Her eyes glittered silver. 'Afraid *you* might be made to look ridiculous for once?'

His mouth was tight as he joined her at the door. 'Where are we going at this time of night?'

'Not far,' she revealed flatly, leading the way over to the lift, her hands becoming clammy as she pressed the button for the top floor, her body tense as it made its smooth ascent.

'Charly, where are we going?' Aaron demanded again tersely.

'This way.' She stepped out of the lift on to the top level of the building, taking him to the door of one of the three luxury apartments on this floor, unlocking the door, pushing it open and stepping back to allow Aaron to precede her inside.

He frowned. 'What the——'

'Go in,' she urged harshly.

He gave her a glittering look before entering the apartment, looking about uninterestedly before turning back to her. 'I don't——'

'Through there.' She nodded towards the door to his right, hanging back herself as he pushed open the door with barely concealed impatience, coming to an abrupt halt just inside the room, the smell of new paint very strong.

For a moment he just stood in stunned silence, then he turned to her with blazing eyes. 'Your bedroom is where?' he demanded gruffly.

'Through the back of this room,' she replied shakily, her own curiosity getting the better of her as she looked into what had once been her comfortably furnished lounge.

The room was empty except for a couple of ladders and some pots of paint, the elegant blue carpet that had once graced the floors taken out along with all the other things that had been burnt in the fire. Some of the wallpaper had been stripped off the walls but the rest of it remained, burnt and scorched, hanging down damply in places where the fire had been put out, the ceiling having black smoke marks streaked across it where the flames had licked against it.

Aaron strode across the room to fling open the door to her bedroom, no sign of the fire in there that had almost taken her life. He closed the door again softly, looking down at the cigarette in his hand before closing his fingers around it and crushing it to ashes.

'Aaron, no———!'

He looked up at her with dark eyes. 'Let's get out of here,' he rasped, grasping her arm to drag her outside and back down to Matt's apartment, closing the door firmly behind them.

'Did you burn your hand just now?' She frowned at him dazedly, stunned by his action.

'You almost died in there and yet you're worried about a little burn on my hand!' he snapped impatiently. 'When do you move back in?' His eyes were narrowed.

'The decorators optimistically claim the week-end,' she answered dully.

He nodded. 'Why don't you move to another apartment building altogether; the thought of going back there obviously disturbs you!'

'I'm surprised you noticed!' she snapped.

'You would be more than surprised if you knew my thoughts most of the time,' he said grimly.

Her mouth tightened. 'I'm moving back to that apartment because it happens to be my home.'

'And what about the house you intend buying so that you can be near Matt?' he accused.

She had thought he was annoyed earlier because she was meeting Matt tomorrow, it seemed it was more than that. 'What house?' she frowned.

'The one that's "completely suitable" and

"convenient", and not too far from the house
Matt shares with Molly so that he can continue to
have the "best of both worlds".' He revealed just
how much of her conversation with Matt he had
overheard—and misunderstood.

'You don't understand——'

'You're wrong, I *do* understand,' he scorned.
'Only too well. You dislike marriage and the
commitment of such a relationship so much that
it doesn't bother you in the least that the man you
want is a married man. You don't even want him
to give up that marriage, are quite content to keep
your independence and him as well. I suppose
the intention is for Matt to spend his time
between the two households.'

'You know Matt, he's your best friend, do you
think he would agree to that?' she dismissed
scornfully.

'He seemd to be trying to fight his attraction
for you—without much success,' Aaron rasped.
'He's meeting you there tomorrow, isn't he?'

'Aaron——'

'*Isn't he?*' he demanded she answer him.

Her eyes flashed. 'I'm not going to be
brow-beaten into admitting something that isn't
true.'

'But you are meeting Matt tomorrow?' he
prompted softly.

'Yes. But——'

'At a house you're purchasing so that you can
be together?'

'No!'

'I heard you, Charly,' he sighed. 'And I don't
want you meeting him there tomorrow or any
other time.'

'Do you really think this is any of your business?' she demanded impatiently.

He nodded. 'It has been since Molly first telephoned me. What do you think this would do to her if she ever found out the truth?'

'I know exactly what it would do to her,' she said bitterly. 'Which is why I agreed to this false engagement to you. But it's all a lie, and this latest idea you have that I intend to set up a little love-nest that Matt can fly to whenever he has a spare moment is ridiculous!' She glared at him. 'I thought I had made it clear that I will never be any man's convenience.'

'Again,' Aaron put in softly.

She gave him a sharp look. 'I beg your pardon?'

'From your attitude towards men and marriage I can only assume I was wrong about your marriage to James Hart being convenient for you, that it was *he* who found the marriage convenient. I take it there was another woman involved?'

'Several,' she acknowledged hardly.

'One of them perhaps serious enough to want to keep him,' Aaron guessed shrewdly.

She nodded. 'Which is why I don't want Molly to get the wrong idea about Matt and me.'

'Because you have no intention of keeping him!' Aaron derided scornfully.

'There is nothing between Matt and me except friendship,' she insisted impatiently.

'Then why was it his apartment you moved into after the fire?'

'Because he only uses the apartment occasionally,' she explained exasperatedly. 'And because he offered.'

'You must have been pretty good friends for him to have made the offer.'

'We knew each other, yes,' she confirmed guardedly, not willing to go into the reasons of their meeting with this man.

'Before or since your widowhood?' Aaron derided.

'Since,' she snapped. 'Look, I'm not on trial here, and I don't have to answer any more of your impertinent questions. It's late, and quite frankly, I have had enough for one day.'

'You're asking me to leave?'

'*Telling* would be a better description.' She looked at him unflinchingly.

He shook his head, his gaze admiring. 'Small chubby blondes may not be in fashion,' he drawled. 'But one small chubby blonde interests me.'

'You can take your interest and——'

'Now, now, Charly.' He took her in his arms, one hand beneath her chin as he lifted her face up to his, taking his time about kissing her. 'Remember, you're a lady,' he taunted. 'A *real* lady.'

His kiss contained all the sensuality of the one they had shared earlier—and more. He coaxed and teased and tempted, until she stood on tiptoe to deepen the caress, groaning low in her throat as his tongue dipped enticingly into her mouth, slowly withdrawing before thrusting inside once again.

His eyes were dark as he looked down at her. 'I have a feeling,' he murmured, 'that you and I are going to be lovers one day.'

She recoiled from the statement, her eyes wide. 'No!'

His mouth twisted as he thrust his hands into his trouser pockets. 'I'm no more thrilled with the idea than you are,' he bit out. 'But I know it's going to happen.'

'Not if it isn't what either of us wants,' she told him determinedly.

'Sometimes we have no control over these things,' he shrugged. 'And maybe if it does happen Matt will see what a fool he's making of himself over you,' he added thoughtfully.

Charly gave him a scornful look. 'I'm surprised you didn't make love to me for that reason alone!'

His eyes narrowed. 'Maybe I would have done if I'd thought of it. But I know it's going to happen anyway.'

Long after he had left Charly sat alone in the lounge with the lights off. Aaron Grantley threatened to destroy the very existence she had made for herself the last year.

CHAPTER FOUR

SHE watched Matt's face as they looked around the house, seeing the excitement in his eyes that he was trying so hard to contain. The house was perfect, she had known it was the moment she first saw it!

'These old places always need a lot of work doing to them,' he murmured. 'The mere fact that there's no heating is going to cause tremendous problems——'

'I've already had the place surveyed and all the estimates for the work that needs doing,' she cut in firmly. 'It's well within the budget I estimated would be necessary.'

He sighed heavily. 'It's a tremendous opportunity, Charly, and don't think I'm not grateful——'

'But?' she prompted softly, sensing the refusal in his voice.

His blue eyes deepened compassionately. 'But I can't accept such a generous gift. I didn't save Stephanie——'

'You tried.' She put her hand on his arm. 'That's all anyone could have asked of you.'

She and Matt had first met just over a year ago across the bed of her unconscious daughter, Matt the one to tell her Stephanie had received serious head injuries, that even if she did regain consciousness she might never recover completely, but if by some miracle she did recover it would be a long, slow process, months spent in hospital.

Charly had seen a lot of Matt during the next two months as he often spent an hour or so with her during the long night hours she sat with her daughter, a bed having been made up for her in the same room as Stephanie. They had talked of everything during those times, had become firm friends, and it had been during that time that Charly had decided she would give this man the hospital he needed to be able to specialise in patients like Stephanie. Not even her daughter's death had changed her mind about that.

Shevton House did need a lot of work and alterations to make it into the relaxed and welcoming atmosphere Matt wanted to work with these long-term patients, but the extensive grounds and secluded cove made it ideal for the therapy activities he had in mind. She knew Matt was aware of that too.

'I can't accept this, Charly,' he told her again stubbornly. 'I was only doing my job.'

'And I want you to continue doing it,' she insisted. 'With the best equipment available.'

'It would cost you millions.' He shook his head.

Charly gave a sad smile. 'I have millions, and no one to spend them on. I'll buy the house even without your agreement,' she added stubbornly. 'I'm sure *someone* would like to use the facilities I intend providing.'

He looked around the beautiful old house that could be made functional as well as comfortable. 'I haven't even discussed it with Molly yet,' he murmured.

'Then do so,' she urged, sensing he was weakening, 'Tell her next weekend while you're away.'

He frowned, indecision still in his face. 'It's a big step to take,' he grimaced. 'Working for a hospital is one thing, going out on my own is something else.'

'When we talked you told me this was your dream in life,' she reminded.

Matt gave a rueful shrug. 'Having a dream and then having you buy it for me are two different things.'

Charly turned angrily to face him. 'In other words it was all just talk, you didn't really want——'

'No, that isn't true,' he shook his head emphatically. 'Dare I say "this is so sudden, Mrs Hart"?' he derided.

Her mouth quirked. 'No, you daren't.'

'Because it isn't,' he acknowledged. 'But I have to admit I didn't think you would come through with your offer.'

Charly frowned at this admission. 'But I said I would.'

'I know,' he sighed. 'But people tend to—I won't say forget, because that wouldn't be true,' Matt frowned. 'But once a patient has left my care, or—or died,' he added regretfully, 'then relatives tend to want to put out of their minds anyone and anything that reminds them of that time.'

She nodded. 'It was a traumatic time, but I promised you the hospital, and I'm going to make sure you get it. I know you weren't able to save Stephanie, but that wasn't your fault,' she told him earnestly. 'And with the facilities I want to provide for you here you'll be able to run one of the best hospitals for injuries of that kind possibly in the world.'

'Staffing it would definitely be no problem,' Matt acknowledged ruefully.

She looked up at him with anxious grey eyes. 'Then you will seriously consider accepting it as a gift?'

He grimaced. 'I'd be a fool to turn it down.'

'I think so, yes,' she confirmed mockingly.

He laughed softly. 'But as most people who know me would tell you, I have been known to be a fool on occasions,' he said dryly.

'And this time?'

'I really don't know, Charly,' he told her truthfully. 'It's a wonderful opportunity, but I do have to talk it over with Molly first, see how it will affect her. You saw what she was like last night, I have to know she could cope with it before I accepted your offer,' he frowned. 'I know that must sound ungrateful——'

'Not at all,' she assured him warmly. 'It sounds exactly like one half of a happy marriage *should* react. It's good to hear.'

'How is the situation with Aaron going?' he asked casually—too casually!

She stiffened. 'He's bossy, overbearing, totally impossible to reason with——'

'And he's very attracted to you,' Matt finished dryly.

She gave him a sharp look, her eyes narrowed. 'He told you?'

'He didn't have to,' his friend derided. 'I've known him long enough to recognise the signs.'

'You mean he's often attracted to women who can't stand him!' Charly scorned.

Matt laughed softly. 'Usually you can't keep the woman away from him.'

'I can see how quite a lot of them would want to do him physical harm!'

'That wasn't quite what I meant,' he chuckled.

'Matt.' She looked at him sternly. 'I hope you don't intend matchmaking between Aaron and me——'

'Good heavens, no,' he dismissed. 'Aaron never has any trouble doing his own attracting.'

'He's out of luck this time,' she scowled.

'He can be quite good fun to be with if you let him,' Matt told her softly.

'I'm not letting him,' she stated firmly. 'Not with me.'

'Hm,' Matt considered. 'Obstinacy on the part of the woman has been known to make him more determined.'

'And giving in to him isn't part of my plans,' she drawled. 'I'd rather be obstinate. And in the meantime I would prefer it if you didn't mention anything about this house or the hospital to him.'

'Why?' Matt was obviously puzzled by the request.

'Because I—I have a competitor for the sale of this house.' She avoided his probing gaze. 'And the less people that know about the deal the better.'

'Aaron can be the soul of discretion.'

Her mouth twisted. 'I have yet to witness that! He still doesn't believe I only moved into your apartment because of the fire in mine, and he's also implied I married James to get control of Hartall Industries,' she recalled hardly.

'Aaron can be a lot of things,' Matt muttered, 'but I've never known him to be this much of an idiot before!'

She gave a derisive smile. 'He seems to have a blind spot where I'm concerned, prefers to believe the worst.'

'He wouldn't if you explained it all to him——'

'No,' she stated firmly. 'Let him go on thinking what he likes about me. I do not want any publicity about my part in the acquisition of this property,' she told him determinedly. 'The press would take delight in splashing a story like this across the front pages of their newspapers. I can almost see the headlines now,' she said bitterly. ' "Allenby-Hart Heiress Buys Hospital for her Dead Daughter's Doctor". I couldn't bear that, Matt,' she shuddered with loathing.

'But it's the truth,' he put in gently.

'Not the way they would write it,' she grimaced. 'I've been the subject of publicity too many times not to know how the press would deal with that information. They could take it two ways, either making it into something sickeningly sentimental, or imply so much into our relationship that no matter how we both denied it, or how much she loves you, Molly would have to wonder if there weren't some truth to the story. The acquisition of this house is to be a private deal, and as soon as possible I will be deeding it over to you. Hopefully no one will ever need to know I was involved,' she dismissed.

'I had thought of calling it the Stephanie Hart Hospital.' Matt looked at her anxiously.

Charly swallowed hard, blinking back the tears. 'I—I'm grateful for the sentiment,' she spoke huskily, 'but I'd rather you didn't.'

'No, perhaps not,' he agreed heavily. 'But I'm sure Aaron would respect the confidence.'

And she was equally sure that if Aaron Grantley knew the reason she was buying Shevton House, that she intended giving it to Matt for his hospital, that he would completely misinterpret the gesture, as he had misinterpreted everything else about the two of them. He did indeed seem to have a blind spot where she was concerned!

'I'd prefer that you didn't tell him,' Charly said with quiet forcefulness. 'Not until something definite has been decided, at least.'

'I can understand that,' Matt nodded. 'And I will talk to Molly about it next weekend.'

She gave an inclination of her head. 'I would be grateful if you would; I really do need an answer as soon as possible.'

She was already confident of what Matt's answer would be, knew Molly was the sort of wife who encouraged her husband's advancement in his career. She was also well aware of what Aaron Grantley would think of her buying Shevton House for Matt; he would think she was trying to buy the other man!

The decorators had finished by the Thursday evening, as they had promised they would, the carpet and new furniture delivered and put in on the Friday, and all that she had to do now was move her things back upstairs. And that was something she was reluctant to do.

She was grateful for the ringing of the doorbell shortly after seven to interrupt her packing, although once she had identified her caller as Aaron Grantley she wasn't quite as pleased.

His gaze raked critically over the clinging

denims and fitted blue cashmere sweater she wore, her hair braided down her spine to keep it out of the way as she worked. She met his gaze challengingly.

'Now you *look* like Charly Allenby,' he finally drawled.

She blinked. 'I beg your pardon?'

'The first night I met you you looked like Matt's mistress, Charly, the next day at your office you were every inch Rocharlle Allenby-Hart,' he recalled dryly. 'That evening too. Now you look like Charly Allenby, a beautiful woman just relaxing at home.' His eyes were dark with appreciation.

She gave him the same slow perusal he had given her, liking the way his own denims fitted snugly to his lean hips and long legs, a tan leather jacket worn over a fitted green shirt. He hardly looked like the board-room barracuda he was either!

'You don't look so bad yourself,' she drawled mockingly.

'Hey, I meant it as a compliment,' he frowned.

'So did I,' she returned straight-faced.

He grimaced ruefully. 'Now I know what it feels like to be "looked over".'

She nodded. 'Not very nice, is it?'

Aaron shrugged. 'Depends who's doing the "looking over", I suppose,' he taunted.

Charly decided that it was time she put an end to this conversation, that it was actually bordering on *flirtatious*. 'What are you doing here?' she demanded to know. 'We aren't due to meet again until next weekend.' She looked at him questioningly. 'Are we? You haven't made any other arrangements for us of which I'm unaware, have you?' Her voice hardened.

His answer was to walk past her and into the apartment, frowning as he saw the boxes she had been packing, his eyes narrowed as he looked back at Charly. 'Going somewhere?'

'Obviously,' she drawled.

'Surely there's legal procedures to go through before you can actually move in?' Aaron rasped.

She frowned her puzzlement. 'Legal procedures?' she repeated. 'If you're talking about the insurance people, they've already been in.' She shook her head in bewilderment.

'Insurance . . .? Charly, where are you going with all this stuff?' he asked slowly.

'Upstairs,' she supplied dazedly. 'Where did you——' Her brow cleared as she realised what he meant. 'Yes, Aaron, there are legal procedures you have to go through before you can buy and move into a house,' she derided.

'Well?'

'Well what?' she taunted.

'Charly, don't play games with me,' he scowled. 'If I hadn't had to go back to the States on business I would have been to see you earlier to find out if Matt approves of the house you picked out for the two of you!'

Charly looked at him with a steady grey gaze. 'He's still thinking about it,' she returned softly.

'Hell, Charly,' Aaron bit out impatiently, 'Matt's a nice guy, but——'

'I think so,' she nodded calmly.

'He's married!' Aaron reminded forcefully.

'I've found that most of the nice ones are,' she returned coolly.

'Charly——'

'*Aaron*! I'm really not in the mood to be lectured by someone who had a much-publicised affair with a senator's wife!' She looked at him challengingly, having made it her business to find out a little bit more about *him* since they last met.

He had the grace to look uncomfortable. 'I didn't have an affair with her,' he denied impatiently. 'I was involved in helping her husband's campaign, and the media made a lot of noise about the fact that I accompanied her to an official dinner when her husband was ill one night.'

Charly gave him a mocking look. 'Isn't it terrible how the most innocent of incidents can be misconstrued?'

He sighed. 'It *was* innocent, Charly.'

'Of course it was,' she humoured him, her eyes wide as he looked at her sharply.

'I can see we aren't going to get anywhere with this conversation,' he dismissed tersely. 'Could I just *ask* you to reconsider before buying a house to be near Matt?' He obviously had to force himself to make it into a request. 'Molly would be sure to realise what was going on eventually.'

Her mouth tightened. 'It's going to be Matt's decision on whether or not I buy the house.'

'No man in his right mind would turn down the opportunity to have you marked private property.'

She shied away from the intensity of his gaze. 'I remember an occasion when you told me the thought of having to make love to me made your skin crawl, and that you would have to be drunk to attempt it!'

He winced as she reminded him of that

conversation. 'I think I may have been a little hasty——'

'I don't,' she cut in briskly. 'And *no* man will ever mark me his "private property!" Now instead of standing there looking useless perhaps you would like to help me take some of these things upstairs?' She considered the idea a brainwave; she didn't particularly want Aaron here, but she dreaded going up to her apartment alone even more.

'You're moving back up to your apartment tonight?' Aaron frowned.

She nodded, putting several more things into boxes; it was amazing how much she had accumulated down here the last week. 'Normally, I would have asked Matt to help me——'

'But as he's having dinner with his in-laws tonight I'll have to do!'

She had had no idea what Matt was doing this evening, but obviously this man was keeping a check on the times they could be together. 'Yes,' she mocked.

He gave her a resentful glare. 'I'm not used to being thought of as a substitute!'

She smiled. 'It must be another terrible blow for your already shattered ego!'

'I doubt if I have one left,' he muttered, picking up two of the boxes. 'Are you coming up with me or do you trust me not to go through your personal things the moment I'm out of your sight?'

She looked at him with steady grey eyes. 'I trust you,' she told him softly.

'That's something at least.' He took the key to her apartment as she held it out to him.

'Just put them in the bedroom,' she requested. 'I'll follow with some more things.'

No matter how annoying she found his behaviour the majority of the time she was grateful for his presence while she reacquainted herself to living in her own apartment again, accepting his help in unpacking the boxes, finding the silence between them strangely companionable.

'That didn't take long,' she thanked him once the last box had been emptied. 'Would you like a cup of coffee?' she offered, still reluctant to be alone up here.

Aaron nodded, having discarded his jacket to fully reveal his muscled arms and chest beneath the green shirt. 'Do you have an apple or something I could eat too?' he requested hopefully.

Her brows rose. 'You haven't had dinner?'

'I came straight to see you once I'd showered and changed,' he shrugged. 'There wasn't time to eat too.'

'And you didn't think you would be staying this long,' she acknowledged ruefully.

'You don't usually make me this welcome,' he agreed dryly.

'You aren't exactly welcome now either.' Her eyes flashed silver. 'But I think you've earnt some dinner.'

'Charly——'

'I won't be long.' She strode into the kitchen without a backward glance, sure he had guessed the reason she had wanted him here tonight.

She didn't need anyone, had deliberately made herself self-sufficient the last year, and she didn't

appreciate Aaron pointing out her weakness
tonight.

'A sandwich will do,' Aaron murmured from
the kitchen doorway as she perused the contents
of her fridge.

She turned to face him. 'I haven't had dinner
either,' she snapped.

'In that case I'll have whatever you're having.'
He wisely left her to it.

She cooked as she did most things, quietly and
efficiently, Aaron hidden behind her newspaper
when she swept through to lay the table. He
lowered it slightly as he heard her moving about
the room, the newspaper rustling back into place
as she looked at him.

'I don't throw things,' she mocked, standing
with her hands on her hips.

The newspaper was slowly lowered again,
green eyes dark with amusement. 'Sure?'

'Yes,' she laughed softly. 'You'll find some
wine in that cupboard over there.' She pointed
across the room.

'You're giving me wine too?' he taunted,
folding the newspaper neatly before putting it
back in the rack. 'What did I do to deserve that?'
He stood up to open the wine cupboard. 'Hm,
what are we having for dinner?' He looked up at
her from his crouching position on the floor.

'Beef.'

'Red wine, then,' he quirked mocking brows at
her. 'Any preferences?'

'Any one will do,' she shrugged. 'I chose them
all personally.'

'A woman that knows what she likes,' he
murmured, studying the contents of the wine

cupboard. 'How about if we forget about red wine and settle for champagne?' He held up a vintage year of Dom Perignon. 'We haven't celebrated our engagement yet.'

'Champagne will be fine, I like sparkling wines,' she said stiffly. 'But I don't think we have anything to celebrate.'

'Possibly not.' He stood up with the bottle of champagne in his hand.

'A bogus engagement to a man I barely know——'

'And have no wish to know,' he put in softly.

'And have no wish to know,' she repeated forcefully. 'Is no cause for celebration!'

'I agree,' Aaron nodded. 'So how would it be if we drank to *getting* to know each other?'

'I'd just like the wine to complement my meal,' she told him sharply. 'For no other reason.' She left to check on the food.

The spaghetti bolognese probably wasn't the beef Aaron had been expecting but it was well-prepared, quick to cook, filling and tasty—and he ate every morsel on his plate, the Italian way. Charly watched in amazement as he twirled the spaghetti neatly on to his fork before popping it neatly into his mouth.

'I have an Aunt Maria who taught me how to appreciate Italian food at an early age,' he explained.

She looked at the trimness of his waist and body. 'It doesn't show,' she mocked.

'Willpower,' he acknowledged. 'Every time I see a pizza or any other Italian dish I think how much exercise I would need to take to run off all the calories, and somehow the temptation isn't there any more.'

'And what reason did you give yourself for giving up smoking?' She patted delicately at the spot of sauce on her chin; unfortunately she didn't have the same expertise with the spaghetti as he did!

He sobered. 'Can't you guess?'

She had noticed he had not had a cigarette the whole evening.

Charly shrugged. 'It can't have been because you can no longer afford it!'

'Every time I even *think* about having a cigarette I remember this room as it was when you showed it to me last.' He looked about the newly decorated room. 'The fact that it was a cigarette that did that much damage scares the hell out of me!'

Her appetite had suddenly faded, and she sipped at her wine to hide her sudden feeling of panic. 'It was an accident,' she dismissed.

'It was damned carelessness,' he scowled. 'And when I thought about it I knew I wasn't always conscious of disposing of my own cigarettes properly.'

'You do it automatically.'

'Your friend didn't,' he reminded grimly. 'I wouldn't ever want to feel I'd been responsible for almost killing someone.'

'So you gave up, just like that?' she frowned, finding it incredible that the fire here should have had such an impact on him.

He grimaced self-derisively. 'I now chew a lot of mints.'

'You'll get fat,' she warned, doubting it was even a possibility; he seemed to be naturally slim.

'Probably,' he agreed ruefully. 'You know, your spaghetti's-a-lika-Aunta-Maria-usa-make.'

Charly laughed at his ham Italian accent. 'Thank you for the compliment.'

'But your method of eating it could do with a little working on,' he mocked as she once again ended up with sauce on her chin. 'Here, let me.' He took her napkin out of her hand, leaning forward—and instead of using the napkin his tongue moved in a silky caress across her chin.

Charly flinched back, glaring at him. 'I'll do it myself, thank you,' she snapped.

He shrugged, completely unperturbed by her anger. 'Then let me show you how to use your spoon and fork so that you at least stop dropping food down your chin.'

She eyed him suspiciously for several seconds, but she couldn't see anything wrong in the suggestion, nodding her agreement. She knew she had been wrong as he stood up to come around the back of her, his body pressed against hers as he showed her the correct way to twirl the spaghetti on to the fork.

He was too close, she could feel the heat of his body on her back, his aftershave spicy, his hands warm as they clasped hers. She didn't want this closeness, had shunned any contact with men the last year, knew she had been right to do so as heat spread through her body, her nipples hardening against the sensuous warmth of her sweater. It was so long since she had known this sexual awareness, if she had ever felt it this strongly before. She couldn't even remember reacting to James' close proximity like this, usually had to be coaxed into lovemaking. Aaron Grantley had merely touched her, and she was so aware of him the colour burnt in her cheeks, her nipples seeming to throb.

'You see,' Aaron murmured against her hair.

'See?' she repeated breathlessly. 'I don't—Oh yes,' she said nervously as he held up the spaghetti on the fork. 'Very nice. But I don't think I'm hungry any more.' She moved restlessly within the confines of his arms, her sexual tension rising. She had to get away from him!

'Charly . . .?' He frowned down at her as he sensed her panic.

She avoided his gaze. 'If you've had enough to eat I'll clear away——'

'Charly!' he groaned now.

Her breathing was ragged and uneven. 'Please. I have to clear away——'

'You aren't going anywhere.' Compelling green eyes held her gaze as he pulled her to her feet in front of him. 'Oh, Charly!' he groaned before his mouth claimed hers, their mouths open to each other, tongues entwining, breaths mingling, Aaron curving her body into his as he showed her how deeply he was aroused.

His hands moved restlessly over her body, each caress too fleeting to be enjoyed to the fullest, Charly beginning to moan her frustration, wanting those leanly sensitive hands on her.

'No!' she pleaded as his hand would have once again left her breast after only the merest of touches, pressing him into her heated flesh. 'Touch me,' she urged, her mouth returning to his.

His caresses warmed her, excited her, their mouths locked together moistly, Charly feeling

her sweater moved aside as Aaron probed
beneath its warmth, cupping beneath the full
weight of her breast, his thumb-tip moving lightly
over the turgid nipple. She had always been
highly sensitised there, and she pressed weakly
against him, begging for more.

Both hands were beneath her sweater now,
caressing rhythmically against her breasts, the
force of his thighs telling her of his own deep
need. She moved to touch him, hearing him gasp
with pleasure as her hand slipped beneath his
clothing to lovingly caress him.

'Oh, Lady. Lady!' he groaned as she continued
to touch him. 'What are you doing to me?'

Her hand began to move, leaving him in no
doubt what she was doing—if indeed he had ever
doubted it. It was as if years of restraint had
suddenly been lifted from her, and she wanted to
share with Aaron all the things she had been too
shy to do with James, wanted to explore the
depths of her own sensuality as well as his.

The deep pile carpet felt soft against her back,
Aaron's weight pressing her down into it; it was a
pleasure-pain that she welcomed, blocking out
the little voice at the back of her head that kept
telling her this was Aaron Grantley, the man who
had been nothing but a torment to her since the
moment she first met him. He was still a torment,
but in a much more pleasurable way.

'I knew you would look like this,' Aaron
groaned, her sweater discarded, her breasts firm,
the nipples darkly brown.

'Please don't stop,' she begged, feeling the
pressure building between her thighs.

'I don't intend to,' he promised, claiming her

lips once more while he caressed beneath her denims. 'You're so moist,' he groaned. 'So ready for me.' He raised his head to look down at her. 'Lady, I need to make love to you, will you let me?'

The way he called her 'Lady' now was so different from that first night, almost like a caress. 'I can't stop you,' she admitted raggedly.

'But will you *let* me?' he persisted.

'I——' she broke off in confusion as the telephone began to ring. Why did they always do that when you least wanted them to!

'Damn!' Aaron seemed no more pleased by the interruption than she was, looking down at her regretfully. 'By the time you've finished taking that call you're going to regret what just happened between us,' he realised ruefully.

She moistened her lips, reaction already setting in, although it wasn't regret for what had happened, it was confusion, need, and a little fear. No—a *lot* of fear!

'I'll get it,' Aaron sighed as the telephone continued to ring, pushing the bottom of his shirt back into his trousers as he crossed the room to pick up the receiver. 'No, Molly, this isn't Charly,' he drawled. 'But I can get her for you.'

Charly had stiffened into a sitting position as soon as the caller identified herself, pushing back the loose tendrils of her hair from her face after pulling on her sweater, her body still deeply aroused. And Aaron Grantley had been the man to excite her to a pitch that she had never known before, not even with James.

'Charly,' he prompted softly, holding out the receiver to her, his hand over the mouth-piece.

She stood up, awkwardly avoiding his gaze. 'Hello, Molly,' her voice was very gruff.

'I haven't interrupted anything, have I?' the other woman sounded concerned. 'I was calling our apartment most of the evening until Matt arrived home and told me you were moving back into your own place tonight, that's why this call is so late,' she apologised.

'What can I do for you?' she asked politely.

'You did say you wouldn't mind going shopping with me some time . . .' Molly sounded uncomfortable. 'Look, I've obviously called at a bad time——'

'You haven't,' she quickly assured her. 'When did you have in mind for the shopping?' She looked round as Aaron disappeared into the kitchen.

'Well my mother has offered to look after the children for me tomorrow, but——'

'Tomorrow sounds fine.' She could hear Aaron opening cupboards in the kitchen, wondering what on earth he was doing in there. 'Would it be easier for you to meet me here or in town?' she asked Molly.

'There, if you wouldn't mind?' Molly agreed eagerly. 'You're sure it's convenient?'

'Very sure.' Charly's brows rose as Aaron came in with a tray of coffee, nodding as he asked if she would like some; the last thing she had expected him to be doing was making coffee! 'About two o'clock, okay?'

'Lovely. I'll see you tomorrow, then,' Molly rang off.

Charly wished the other woman hadn't ended the conversation quite so abruptly, slowly replacing her own receiver. 'Thank you for the coffee.' She wearily sank down into the chair opposite Aaron, the two of them sitting in silence for several minutes.

'I know this is the part where you're supposed to protest at my seduction of you.' Aaron finally spoke, his eyes a dark slumbrous green, his dark hair tousled on to his forehead. 'But that wouldn't be true, would it?' he watched her intently.

She took a sip of her coffee, gasping as it burnt her top lip. 'Maybe *I* should be apologising for seducing you?' she suggested self-derisively, knowing she had been the aggressor in the encounter.

His mouth twisted. 'That wouldn't be true either.'

'Then what is true?' she asked sharply.

'That we want each other,' he shrugged. 'That we have a need of each other.'

'It isn't enough for—for what just happened,' she snapped.

'Surely it's better than that unhappy marriage you had with James Hart?' he demanded angrily. 'At least we genuinely want each other and wouldn't be making love out of duty!'

'I never made love with James out of duty!' Her eyes flashed warningly.

'Never?' he taunted softly.

'Never,' she insisted defiantly.

'Never once cried off with a non–existent headache?' Aaron mocked.

Embarrassment coloured her cheeks. 'It is possible to have a genuine headache,' she defended.

'Charly, we want each other,' he told her intensely. 'You can't stop the fact that sooner or later we are going to make love.'

She stood up. 'Thank you for helping me bring my things up here this evening.'

'End of conversation?' he derided.

She nodded. 'End of conversation.'

Aaron shrugged, standing up too. 'You didn't appear to me to be a woman who would hide from the truth when confronted with——'

'I'm not hiding from anything!' She handed him his jacket. 'I'm well aware of the fact that I'm attracted to you,' she snapped. 'I just don't intend doing anything about it.'

'Again,' he taunted.

Charly's mouth tightened. 'Tonight was un-fortunate——'

'And your choice of word is *unfortunate*,' he ground out hardly, taking hold of her chin roughly. 'I'm going to keep working on you, Lady, until you have to give in.'

She turned her face away, only to have it wrenched back by his hand on her chin. 'Take your hands off me,' she ordered through gritted teeth, breathing heavily. 'And don't go away with the idea that today was a foretaste of what's to come; I have always been in control of my actions.' Until now, a little voice in her head mocked. A voice she ignored.

'Then you've slipped up badly tonight,' Aaron mocked. 'Because now that I've seen what it's like between us I'm not going to make do with anything less than all of you. You may think I don't have the choice, but I've never given up on anything I wanted as badly as I want you. Matt may be my best friend, but he's going to find himself ousted from your life so quickly he'll wonder if he was ever in it!'

'That much confidence is going to leave you looking rather stupid,' Charly scorned.

'You don't love Matt,' Aaron stated arrogantly.

Her mouth tightened. 'I like him better than any other man I know!'

'Including me.'

'Especially you!'

He looked at her mockingly. 'Don't worry, I'm not going to settle for any half-hearted emotion such as liking.' He leant forward and lightly kissed her forehead. 'I'm going to want a complete surrender.'

'You won't get it from me!' she spat the words.

He shrugged. 'I'll call for you late Friday afternoon. We won't need both cars, so you might as well drive down with me,' he told her firmly as she looked about to protest. 'Independence is fine in its right place, Charly, but I'd like a little more togetherness in future.'

'*You* would like?' she repeated indignantly, stepping back, anger her only defence when she was feeling so exposed emotionally. 'I really don't care what you would like or dislike,' she flared at him. 'Now would you please leave?'

'Of course I'll leave, you didn't think I was about to overstay my welcome, did you?' he taunted.

Her head went back. 'You did that the moment you arrived!'

'You didn't seem to think so at the time,' he drawled. 'In fact, you seemed quite pleased to see me.'

She blushed as she realised the truth of his words. 'And now I want you to leave.'

'I'm going,' he smiled. 'After all, we have all of next weekend together for me to look forward to.'

She closed the door behind him with more force than was strictly necessary, anger at herself making her angry with him. There had been men, a lot of men since James died, who had tried to induce desire where none existed; Aaron hadn't even tried, it had just been there for him. She had thought she disliked him, that his erroneous assumptions about her and Matt made her despise him. It hadn't been dislike she felt for him tonight.

And she could still feel that fear licking through her body, fear that her dependence on Aaron Grantley could be completely different from her emotional need of James at the beginning of their marriage. She wasn't sure which was worse, the emotional or physical need. Or which was going to hurt her the worst.

One thing she did know, her nervousness about sleeping in the apartment because of the fire had completely gone now, no longer imagining smoke and flames in the lounge, haunted by a much more vivid picture of her in Aaron's arms on the carpet as they made love!

And it was that memory that made her run to the peace and protection of her bedroom.

CHAPTER FIVE

'I KNEW there was a reason I didn't shop in London very often.' Molly collapsed into the chair opposite Charly in the restaurant, the two of them having ordered a reviving pot of tea.

Charly smiled. 'It is exhausting.' She had forgotten herself just *how* exhausting, rarely finding the time to brave the shops of London herself any more, not even for clothes, having her dressmaker send over a selection for her to choose from. But it had been a pleasant change to enjoy the relaxed company of another woman as they browsed through the clothes shops, Molly finding several new dresses.

They both smiled gratefully at the waiter as he brought their tea, Charly leaving it to Molly to pour.

'Now you really must tell me all about you and Aaron,' Molly invited avidly.

She couldn't say she was exactly surprised by the question, but that hadn't really helped her find any answers; she knew little or nothing about Aaron's likes and dislikes. 'What do you want to know?' She stirred the milk into her tea, her gaze evasive.

'Oh not much,' Molly shrugged ruefully. 'Just where you met? How long you've known each other? How long have you been in love?'

'Just a few facts, then?' Charly derided.

Molly laughed. 'Yes.'

She shrugged. 'We met at a party a couple of months ago.' She felt the generality was pretty safe. 'The last time Aaron was in England,' she added for effect.

'In August?' Molly frowned. 'But he was only in the country overnight.'

Charly laughed dismissively. Rule number one, she must remember not to enlarge on an already accepted answer! 'You're right, that visit was so fleeting I'd forgotten about it,' she nodded. 'I meant the time before that, of course.'

'June,' Molly nodded. 'He certainly kept quiet about you for a long time.'

'That was my fault, I'm afraid.' She really would have to find out more about Aaron Grantley before being caught in a conversation like this again! 'I'm a little cautious about relationships since my marriage.'

'Aaron explained about your husband dying; it must have been so sad for you,' Molly sympathised.

'Yes,' she answered abruptly.

'But now you and Aaron have found happiness together.' The other woman brightened. 'I can hardly wait for the wedding!'

'It is sure to be an event,' Charly agreed wryly.

'Aaron has asked Matt to be his best man.' Molly told her in a pleased voice.

Charly stiffened. 'He's what?' she gasped.

'Well it is a little premature yet, with no date having been set,' the other woman acknowledged. 'Aaron explained that,' she nodded. 'But he asked Matt anyway.'

'I see,' she bit out, wishing she did 'see'! Surely this was taking the pretence too far!

'I suppose it will be a church wedding?' Molly asked curiously. 'Aaron said you would both prefer it.'

Charly frowned. 'When did he say that?'

'He called over late yesterday afternoon to see the children on his way from viewing a property he's interested in buying, and he was still there when Matt got home. I would have thought he would have mentioned it when he came over last night.' She sounded surprised that he hadn't.

'It was late when he got there,' Charly hastily excused. 'And we had to move my things back upstairs; we didn't get a chance to talk about the wedding at all.' But she had an idea the property Aaron had been viewing yesterday afternoon had been Shevton House!

'Aaron is so much in love,' Molly said indulgently. 'He can't wait for the two of you to be married.'

'I'm looking forward to it myself,' she said through gritted teeth. 'But there are still a lot of the details to be worked out.'

'Where you're going to live for one thing,' Molly teased.

'That is a problem,' she agreed non-committally, not going to fall into that trap a second time.

'The country is nicer,' Molly nodded. 'But I realise London would be more convenient for you.'

That hadn't been exactly what she thought the problem might be in such a marriage, but as Molly seemed to be assuming she and Aaron would live in England she realised she had been right to be cautious; she had no way of knowing *what* Aaron had told the other woman.

'It is,' she nodded.

'It will be lovely having Aaron living closer; we see so little of him at the moment. Not that we'll expect to see much of either of you the first few months,' she teased. 'There's something about being just married.' She gave a whimsical smile. 'Matt and I lived together for a year before we got married, and yet even so it was a magical time after we were married. I think it's the total commitment that does it, the *knowing* that you want to be together.' She gave a rueful smile. 'It seems strange to think of myself as the student-nurse I was then. Especially now I'm expecting our third child.'

'How do you feel about that now you've had chance to get used to the idea?' Charly prompted gently.

'Still shocked, but resigned. And I don't mean that in a bad way,' she hastened to explain. 'It's just that the baby is a fact, so we have to accept it, and look forward to its birth. I'm getting quite excited actually,' she confided. 'Aaron told me the two of you would like three or four children yourselves.'

Now he had gone too far! It was all right talking about mythical engagements, even mythical weddings, but mythical *children* was just too much!

'I think wanting and actually having are two different things,' she evaded.

'Aaron will make a very good father,' Molly told her thoughtfully.

Surprisingly enough, she believed he would too! He would be firm but not strict, under-standing rather than uninterested, teasing rather than overindulgent. But he would never father any children by her!

He could at least have warned her of his visit to Molly yesterday, and of the subsequent intimate revelations he appeared to have made about their imagined future together.

'He's marvellous with our two,' Molly added lightly. 'Are you really going to give him complete control of Tommy next weekend?' she teased.

'If you wouldn't mind?' she nodded.

'I don't mind,' Molly smiled. 'Men can be so complacent about coping with children. They spend a couple of hours with them on a Saturday and Sunday, and then can't understand why some days you're at screaming pitch after being with them all day.' She shook her head. 'I think I should let *you* in on the little secret I have for getting Tommy to sleep, though,' she said ruefully. 'Even Matt doesn't know what it is; he thinks I've performed a miracle when I get the little monkey to sleep in minutes when he's been trying all evening!'

Charly returned the other woman's smile. 'Aaron is convinced he'll succeed where you've failed.'

'Not without my secret he won't,' Molly said with certainty.

'Then by all means let me in on the secret,' she urged.

'It's simple really, you just sit in the rocker with him in your arms and gently sing "The Lullaby Song". Do you know the one I mean?'

She nodded stiffly. 'It used to be a favourite of Stephanie's. My daughter,' she explained abruptly.

Molly frowned. 'Then perhaps I ought to let Aaron in on the secret after all; it will be too painful for you.'

'Not at all,' she shook her head firmly. 'I'll enjoy holding and singing to a baby again. Besides,' she lightened the conversation, 'it won't hurt Aaron to suffer a little.'

'What's he done to upset you?' Molly giggled.

'Nothing. But he might consider bringing the number of children down from three or four to just one!'

Molly chuckled. 'Men have very short memories when it comes to the unpleasant things in life, such as irritable children.'

'Yes,' Charly agreed ruefully. 'Well, I suppose we ought to be making a move.' The pot of tea was empty, the sandwiches and cakes eaten. 'You have to get back, and I have a date this evening. With Aaron,' she added hastily.

'Who else?' Molly dismissed, motioning for the bill.

Who else, indeed! Bill Shaw was a business acquaintance who would like to be much more, and Charly had arranged to have dinner with him before she entered into this bogus engagement with Aaron. And she had no intention of cancelling dinner with the pleasant man Bill was because of that.

But before she went on her date with Bill she intended paying Aaron a visit at his hotel. There was really no need for him to complicate matters with a lot more lies, and she was going to tell him so before things went any further.

She insisted on paying for the tea before she and Molly went outside.

'Maybe we can do this again some time,' Molly suggested as she unlocked her parked car outside the apartment building. 'Once you and Aaron have settled down.'

She and Aaron would never settle down—at least, not together! 'I'd like that,' she nodded, waving to the other woman as she drove away.

Her smile faded as soon as the car drove out of sight. Damn Aaron Grantley! He had turned a pleasant afternoon's shopping into a fiasco, as she headed off one claim after another that he had made to Molly only yesterday afternoon!

She was still angry when she got into her car later that evening, unaware of how attractive she looked with the flush to her cheeks, her gown the same shimmering silver as her eyes, her hair plaited and coiled in a golden crown about her head. She looked regal as she parked the car in front of the hotel, leaving the key with the doorman, too angry to be aware of the admiring glances following her progress across the lobby to the reception desk.

'Tell Mr Grantley I'm on my way up,' she informed the male receptionist, surreptitiously watching the room number he dialed. 'Rocharlle Allenby-Hart,' she supplied as the man looked at her enquiringly. Aaron was in room seven-one-seven! 'Don't bother,' she instructed the man. 'I've decided I'd like to surprise him after all,' she gave him a friendly smile.

The man hastily put down the receiver as she turned and walked towards the lift. 'Miss Hart—er—Allenby-Hart!' he amended, following her.

She turned slowly, one brow raised in haughty enquiry. 'Yes?' she drawled arrogantly.

The man moistened his lips nervously. 'I really should inform Mr Grantley you're here before allowing you up.'

'Very well.' She gave a haughty inclination of her head. 'But you'll ruin the surprise.'

He looked even less confident. 'Surprise?'

Charly gave him a dazzling smile. 'Yes— surprise,' she drawled provocatively.

'Oh.' The man coloured with embarrassment. 'Er—Okay,' he beat a hasty retreat back to his desk.

Charly's mouth tightened once the lift doors had closed. Aaron Grantley was going to get a surprise, all right, but she wasn't sure it was one he would like!

Her foot tapped impatiently on the carpeted corridor as she waited for him to open the door to her knock, the three-inch heels on her sandals giving her legs a slender elegance. Only the slight widening of her eyes showed she was put off-guard as Aaron opened the door wearing only a towel draped about his hips, a second towel about his neck as he wiped the excess shaving-foam off his recently shaved chin.

He didn't look in the least surprised to see her, and Charly could only assume he had already identified his caller through the small peep-hole in the door. She wished she had thought to put her hand over it!

'Well can I come in?' she asked waspishly. 'Or do you always keep women standing outside your door like this?'

His mouth quirked as he stepped back to let her enter the comfortably luxurious suite. 'Not my bedroom door, anyway,' he drawled.

'I'm sure,' she derided coldy. 'I——' she broke

off as she saw the pretty redhead seated in the lounge for the first time, her brows rising questioningly as she turned back to Aaron.

'Charly, this is Erin Brody,' he introduced calmly, not in the least perturbed by her arrogance. 'Erin, this is Rocharlle Allenby-Hart. Charly to her friends,' he added with a grin. 'And as her fiancé I think I must qualify as that,' he said goadingly.

Her mouth tightened. 'Miss Brody,' she greeted abruptly.

'Nice to meet you,' the other woman nodded, smiling openly, American, like Aaron. 'I had no idea you were engaged, Aaron.' She looked at him curiously.

He shrugged, seeming not to care that he had just greeted his supposed fiancée wearing only a towel when he had been alone in the suite with another woman. 'Charly doesn't actually believe in engagements,' he dismissed. 'But we are getting married.'

'Congratulations,' the younger woman said warmly.

Aaron arched mocking brows at Charly's puzzled look. 'I think I forgot to mention that Erin is my secretary,' he drawled, triumphant humour in emerald eyes. 'That's all for tonight, Erin,' he told the younger woman. 'We'll continue in the morning.'

'Secretary?' Charly derided softly once Erin had taken her leave, the other woman, with her voluptuous figure, looking the least like a secretary that she had ever seen. 'At least James used to tell me they were business acquaintances!' she scorned.

Aaron shrugged. 'Erin *is* my secretary. I like to have beautiful women around me.'

'So did James.'

His face darkened at this second mention of her husband. 'Don't keep comparing me with a husband you obviously despised,' he rasped.

Her head went back proudly. 'Why not? You're very much alike.'

'I doubt that,' he bit out. '*I* would never have treated you in the way he obviously did.'

Charly's mouth twisted. 'So you're sticking to the story that Erin is *just* a secretary?'

'It isn't a story, and it happens to be the truth as far as I'm concerned. What she does with other men is none of my concern. She has a brother who plays professional football who would probably rearrange my face if I so much as looked at her suspiciously,' he grimaced.

Charly sighed. 'Don't try and make me laugh. I'm angry with you and I want to stay that way!'

He pulled a face. 'In that case I think I'd better go and put some clothes on before we continue this conversation; I have a feeling the argument you're spoiling for might go more in my favour if I looked a little more dignified!'

'By all means get dressed,' she invited impatiently, preferring not to have to look at his bare muscled chest any longer anyway. 'But don't be long, I have to leave in a few minutes.'

His eyes narrowed to hard slits. 'Am I to take that to mean you didn't get dressed up like that just to see me?'

'Of course I didn't,' she snapped, sitting down, crossing one silky covered leg over the other.

'Then who's it for?' His eyes were still narrowed.

'None of your damned business,' she bit out coldly.

His expression darkened. 'We'll continue this conversation when I get back!'

Charly slumped down in the chair slightly once he had gone into the bedroom, wishing she had a drink at that moment, knowing she would have had a cigarette if she didn't hate the damned things so much. Because for a moment, a very brief moment, jealousy such as she had never known before had wracked her body as she looked at Erin Brody in Aaron's suite with him!

Jealousy! She couldn't believe it, still felt devastated by the realisation that she had hated the thought of Aaron being with any other woman but her. She didn't even like the man, but after yesterday night she knew that she wanted him!

'Charly, I—Are you all right?' Aaron frowned as he came back into the room, and Charly realised she must have gone pale as she admitted to herself that her physical need of this man hadn't just been for last night.

'Of course I am,' she snapped a reply, glaring at him. 'I spent the afternoon with Molly listening to how Matt is going to be your best man, we're having a church wedding, and three or four children!'

'Ah,' he nodded understandingly. 'You're a little annoyed, right?'

'I'm a *lot* annoyed! Although *annoyed* doesn't really begin to describe how I feel about it!' she bit out, her anger at her attraction to him in spite of herself also contained in this exchange. 'You could at least have warned me!' she accused.

'I did mean to,' he assured her slowly. 'But somehow we got sidetracked last night.'

She avoided his gaze at the mention of last night. 'You shouldn't have told them those things in the first place!'

Aaron shrugged. 'It just seemed to come out so naturally. Molly was very pleased for us.'

'Well *I'm* not!' She glared up at him.

'Okay, I'll try and avoid conversations like that in future,' he dismissed, his eyes narrowing. 'Now you can tell me who you're meeting tonight?'

'A business acquaintance,' she dismissed.

'Dressed like that?' he scorned.

Her eyes flashed silver. 'There's nothing that says I can't look nice to meet a business acquaintance!'

'There is—*me*!' he bit out. 'I don't want you meeting another man looking like that.'

'Well that's just too bad, because there's nothing wrong with the way I look!'

'I'm well aware of that,' he rasped. 'Which is why I don't think you're going to any business meeting——'

'I didn't say I was,' she cut in coldly. 'Just that I know the man *through* business.'

'You aren't going!'

Her eyes flashed. 'I am!'

'You're supposed to be marrying me!' His mouth was tight.

She gave a scornful laugh, standing up. 'We both know that isn't true, so I'm at liberty to see who I please, when I please.'

'You didn't seem to feel the same way about Erin being here with me earlier,' he taunted.

She avoided his probing eyes. 'I couldn't care

less what women you see, but it might not have been me at the door,' she pointed out desperately, knowing she had hated the thought of him making love to the other woman.

'Is that the only reason you were so annoyed at seeing her here?' he mocked.

'Of course,' she snapped. 'You don't seriously think I *minded* for myself, do you?' she derided.

'I know damn well you did,' he mocked.

Her mouth firmed into a thin line. 'I think you were wrong the other day, Aaron, your ego is still very much intact—in fact, it's running wild! Now if you'll excuse me, I have a date.'

Aaron grasped her arm. 'Who is he?'

Her eyes flashed. 'None of your business!'

'Tell me, Charly,' he ordered in a softly threatening voice.

She hadn't seen him this angry since the first night when he arrived at Matt's apartment to accuse her of being his mistress. 'If you must know,' she began contemptuously.

'Oh I think I must,' he drawled mockingly.

'His name is William Shaw.'

'Of Shaw Electronics?'

She looked at him sharply. 'Do you know him?' That would be just her luck the way things were going lately!

To her relief Aaron shook his head. '*Of* him. So,' he released her, stepping back, 'does Matt know you see other men on the evenings you don't see him?' he bit out.

Her mouth twisted. 'Why don't you ask him?'

'Because I'm asking you,' he rasped.

She shrugged. 'I doubt if he knows about Bill,' she answered truthfully.

'Or vice versa,' Aaron derided.

'Bill wouldn't be interested in Matt,' she answered, again with complete honesty.

Aaron frowned. 'Don't you find your life a little—complicated, the way it is?'

She gave him a haughty look. 'I like my life exactly the way it is. Or rather, I *liked* it.'

'Before I came along to spoil it,' he guessed dryly.

'You're the only complication I can see,' she nodded, looking down at the slender gold watch on her wrist. 'I'm late,' she realised irritably.

'Why not call him and tell him you'll be there soon?' Aaron suggested mildly.

Charly eyed him suspiciously. 'What are you up to now?'

'Nothing.' He moved across the room to pour himself a drink. 'I just thought you might like to ring his home and explain that you'll be late.'

'He isn't at home.' She still frowned at Aaron's helpful about-face. 'We're meeting at the restaurant.'

He shrugged. 'Then call the restaurant.'

'Aaron——'

'If you don't want to, fine,' he dismissed. 'I was only trying to be helpful.'

'Why?'

'Because you're late for your date——'

'A date you were trying to stop me going on a few minutes ago!' she reminded hardly.

'I realised you're right, it's none of my business.' He met her stormy gaze with calm green eyes.

She was still wary of the reasons for his sudden change of attitude, but she made the call to the restaurant anyway, Bill coming on the line a couple of minutes later. She explained that a friend had dropped by unexpectedly and she had been delayed, avoiding Aaron's mocking gaze as she assured Bill she would be at the restaurant shortly.

'I have to leave now,' she told Aaron once she had rung off. 'Thanks for the use of the telephone.'

'Any time,' he nodded.

'And I really would appreciate it if you didn't embellish our relationship to Molly any further.'

'Fine,' he nodded again.

'Aaron, what are you up to?' she snapped demandingly, hesitating in the act of leaving.

'Me?'

His look of a feigned innocence convinced her more than ever that he was up to something. 'Aaron——'

'You really should be going, Charly,' he suggested mildly. 'You did say fifteen minutes,' he reminded.

'Yes,' she still frowned suspiciously. 'I'll see you next weekend.'

'If not before,' he nodded.

She gave him a sharp look. 'And what do you mean by that?' she looked at him warily.

Aaron shrugged. 'Well there's always the possibility that I might need to see you before for some reason. But don't worry,' his voice hardened, 'I'll call you first.'

She stiffened. 'There's no need.'

His gaze was steady on her flushed face. 'I'll call first,' he stated flatly.

Charly knew he was implying he didn't want to

call at her apartment without her knowledge in case she had Matt there, taking her leave abruptly.

But she still wasn't convinced by his suddenly helpful mood, his air of innocence, a frown marring her brow all the way to the restaurant.

CHAPTER SIX

SHE didn't know why she was surprised to see Aaron enter the restaurant about fifteen minutes after she had, Erin Brody at his side. But she was. And her surprise must have shown in her face, Bill turning round to follow her line of vision.

'Do you know them?' He looked back at Charly.

She dragged her stunned gaze away as Aaron and Erin were seated at a table a short distance away from them. 'Yes,' she confirmed abruptly, furiously wondering how Aaron had known it was this particular restaurant she was meeting Bill at; she felt sure she hadn't mentioned the name of it during her telephone conversation with Bill earlier.

'Rocharlle?'

She looked up guiltily, knowing she had missed something Bill said. 'Sorry?'

'I asked if you would like them to join us?' he offered politely.

'No! Er—I'm sure they would rather be on their own,' she spoke more calmly, giving him a dazzling smile. 'As we would.'

Bill looked visibly taken aback by this intimate warmth. As well he might! He had been trying to persuade her for months to go out to dinner with him, and even when she had finally agreed it had been with some reluctance. No wonder he was surprised by her flirtatious manner now. She had a feeling he was going to be a lot more surprised by her behaviour before the evening was finished, Aaron's arrogance in following her here bringing out a rebellious streak in her. Because he had followed her, the coincidence of being here was just too great for it to be otherwise.

She felt herself stiffen as she saw Aaron getting to his feet and coming towards their table, keeping her eyes averted as she sensed him standing beside her.

'What a coincidence,' he said with obvious insincerity—at least, it was obvious to Charly, Bill seemed completely convinced by the act. 'I had no idea it was this restaurant you were going to, Charly.'

'Charly?' Bill was surprised by the nickname.

She shot Aaron an impatient look before turning to the other man. Until tonight Bill had remained purely a business acquaintance, and in business she always preferred the formality of being Rocharlle Allenby-Hart; who could take a woman called Charly seriously in business! 'Just a shortened version of my name,' she dismissed, doubtful if this man would ever be more than a 'business acquaintance'.

Aaron nodded, a wicked gleam in his eyes. 'Charly and I are old friends.'

Bill stiffened, a man in his early forties, silver gleaming in his thick dark hair, a look of cynicism to his handsome face. 'Oh?' he prompted warily.

'Very old friends,' Aaron antagonised.

'I believe Erin is feeling neglected,' Charly told him through stiff lips.

He turned to glance at the other woman, Erin giving a little wave of acknowledgement as she saw that glance. 'She looks happy enough to me,' he mocked. 'Actually I came over to see if you would care to join us?'

Charly's mouth tightened even more. 'I don't think so, thank you,' she glared at him warningly.

'Why not?' he asked bluntly.

Colour darkened her cheeks. 'Because I'm sure the two of you would rather be alone,' she snapped.

'Not particularly,' he shrugged. 'Besides, how *can* you be alone in a crowded restaurant?'

She gave an impatient sigh. 'Bill and I have business to discuss.'

'You can discuss it later,' Aaron told her arrogantly. 'Come on, Charly,' he encouraged throatily. 'It's been so long since we saw each other.'

She held on to her temper with effort at his deliberate goading of her. 'Bill?' she prompted abruptly.

He looked no more pleased, now he had heard the familiar way Aaron spoke to her, with the arrangement. 'I have no objections, but it would be an inconvenience for the management if we were to change tables now,' he added with relief.

'Not at all,' Aaron contradicted smoothly. 'In case you haven't noticed, Erin and I are at a table for four.'

Charly looked up at him accusingly, sure that fact hadn't come about as casually as Aaron was implying it had. 'In that case . . .' she muttered. 'Bill?'

'Of course.' He stood up, holding her chair back for her, the waiter carrying their cocktails to the other table.

Aaron made the introductions as they all sat down, Charly somehow finding herself seated between Erin and Aaron, giving Bill a helpless look as he looked less than pleased at being seated across the table from her.

It was an awkward meal for everyone except Aaron, who seemed unaffected by Charly's scowls, Bill's displeasure, and Erin's puzzlement, talking about everything and nothing, drawing Bill into a business discussion.

Charly could cheerfully have hit him, was furiously angry with both him and Bill by the time they reached the coffee stage of their meal, seriously considering walking out on them as she returned from the ladies' room.

'That would only embarrass Erin and Bill,' Aaron drawled.

She turned furiously to find him leaning against the wall in the entrance area. 'And whose fault would that be?' she demanded. 'You had no right following me here.'

'I didn't follow you,' he told her calmly.

'Then how did you know I would be at this restaurant?' she scorned.

'What makes you think I did know?' he enquired with a pained innocence.

'Because these sort of coincidences didn't happen to me until you came into my life!' she hissed, lowering her voice as some people entered the restaurant behind them.

'What a boring life you must have led until I came along,' Aaron drawled.

'How-did-you-know-which-restaurant-I-would-be-at?' she asked again with controlled violence.

He shrugged, bending his head guiltily. 'Okay, I'll confess——'

'And stop trying to look and act like a naughty boy caught out in a misdemeanour,' she snapped. 'It's ridiculous in a man of thirty-four.'

'Thirty-five,' he corrected.

'It's ridiculous in a grown man whatever his age.' Her eyes flashed.

Aaron grinned. 'But cute, huh?'

'It is not cute!'

'You know I'm beginning to think that something was left out of your expensive education,' he frowned.

'Oh yes?' she scorned.

'A sense of humour,' he taunted. 'It can help you through a lot of awkward occasions.'

'No doubt you've had great need of your *warped* sense of humour over the years!'

'Not nice,' he reproved. 'Okay,' he shrugged. 'I can see you definitely aren't amused. It was the telephone number that brought me here.'

She frowned. 'What telephone number?'

'This telephone number, of course.' His voice was edged with impatience.

She shook her head. 'I know for a fact that I didn't mention this telephone number.'

'I watched you dial. I have a good memory for numbers, and this was an easy one to remember. As soon as you left my suite I called here and made my own reservation, with a table for four, of course.'

'How enterprising of you,' she bit out, annoyed that he had used the same subterfuge she had when obtaining the number of his hotel room.

'I thought so,' he nodded.

'Well, now that you've had your little game could Bill and I leave?' she said with sarcasm.

'Bill and you, sure. But if you walk out of here alone—as you were thinking of doing just now—you'll only embarrass Bill and Erin. That is, unless they've already left,' he added softly.

Charly gave him a sharp look. 'What do you mean by that?'

'Haven't you noticed the way they've been looking at each other all evening? They're attracted to each other.'

She frowned, having noticed nothing. 'You're imagining things,' she scoffed.

'I'm not,' he shook his head confidently. 'Perhaps you were too interested in me to notice them.'

'I don't think so,' she drawled derisively.

'No, perhaps not,' he conceded dryly. 'But I know Erin well enough to realise when she likes a man, and Bill Shaw seems to return the interest. I hope you aren't too upset about it?' he taunted.

She bit her tongue to stop herself denying being in the least affected by Bill Shaw's interest in Erin or any other woman. Last night she had almost made love with this man; it was better for her defences if he continued to believe he was only one of many in her life instead of the only man to affect her in that way since the beginning of her marriage to James. She had enough complications in her life without Aaron Grantley knowing he was the first man she had been physically attracted to in years!

'Perhaps if you hadn't insisted on monopolising quite so much of my attention they wouldn't have found the time to become attracted to each other,' she said coldly.

Aaron's eyes widened. 'You *are* upset.'

She looked at him unflinchingly. 'What did you expect me to be?'

'You didn't seem that interested in him earlier,' he frowned.

'I'm not a very demonstrative person.' Her icy gaze dared him to dispute that claim. He didn't. And she didn't know if she was angry or relieved that he didn't! After last night he had to know she could be *very* demonstrative, but she didn't want him to talk about that time she had spent in his arms. And yet she didn't like the idea of him perhaps not realising how deeply she had been aroused. It was a no-win situation, and she impatiently dismissed it from her mind. 'But if you don't mind, we'll leave now.' It was a statement, not a request.

Bill gave her a curious look once they returned to the table, and she couldn't help wondering if her cheeks were as red as their heat implied they were.

'Sorry to be so long,' Aaron told the other couple cheerfully. 'Once Charly and I start talking about old times we forget the time.' He looked at her challengingly.

She didn't resume her seat back at the table. 'Bill, are you ready to leave now?' she asked tightly.

He looked startled by the request. 'It's early yet,' he frowned. 'Erin and I were just discussing going on somewhere to dance.'

Her mouth tightened. 'I'm not in the mood for dancing.'

'Neither am I,' Aaron said with satisfaction. 'So I'll go home with Charly and you can take Erin dancing,' he told the other man.

'Oh, I couldn't let you do that.' Bill shook his head. 'Rocharlle is here with me; I'll drive home with her.'

Although politely made the offer was none the less reluctant. 'I have my car and can take myself home, thank you,' she snapped, her eyes flashing silver, looking from Aaron to Bill and then back again. 'I'm not some simpleton who needs an escort home.'

'That isn't very nice, Charly.' Green eyes danced with fun at her anger, and she realised that by showing her anger at Bill as well as Aaron she had played into the latter's hands.

She turned to Bill with a warm smile. 'I really would like to go home now, I have a headache,' she told him softly. 'But please feel free to take Erin dancing,' her smile included the younger woman, 'I really don't need an escort for the short drive home.'

'I think I'll come with you anyway.' Aaron mocked the fact that he had been right about the other couple's attraction to each other.

Her eyes frosted over, her smile fading. 'I'd rather go alone.'

He shrugged. 'Okay, I'll see you at the apartment later.'

She felt herself pale even as she gasped, glancing worriedly at Bill. 'Don't be silly, Aaron,' she dismissed lightly, 'of course you won't be seeing me at my apartment later.' She gave the stunned Bill a reassuring smile.

'Sweetheart, this argument of ours is ridiculous,' he told her cajolingly, satisfaction gleaming in his eyes. 'I told you earlier that Erin is only my secretary.'

So he had persuaded the other woman to come along with him by telling her she had left in a jealous huff! She had wondered how he persuaded Erin to go along with his plan after telling her they were engaged.

'Earlier?' Bill looked even more puzzled. 'Rocharlle, I don't understand what's going on?'

She gave a defeated sigh. 'I'm sure Aaron will explain everything to you once I've left!' She turned and walked out of the room without a backward glance, although she sensed admiring green eyes following her every move.

Damn the man. He had completely ruined her evening with a pleasantly interesting man, and she hated to think what lies he was now telling Bill. She hadn't thought there would be such repercussions from her initial vengeful announcement to Molly only a week ago. By this time tomorrow, with Bill obviously told of the bogus engagement, the whole of the business-world would know about it!

'Slow down!' Aaron caught up with her just as she got out on to the pavement, holding on to her arm.

She shook off his hand. 'You deliberately made a fool of me in there!' she bit out through clenched teeth.

'I didn't need to,' he drawled. 'You managed that quite well on your own!'

'Why you——'

'Charly, you're so confused right now you don't know what you want,' he chided.

'I've always despised women who claim to be confused all the time!' she snapped.

'You aren't confused all the time,' he teased. 'Just right now. You don't know whether to be mad at me for following you to the restaurant, because I had Erin with me, or because I told Bill we're engaged.'

She looked at him fiercely. 'I'm mad at you for all those things. You made me look like a spitefully jealous child to Erin and a confused idiot to Bill. And I'm not used to being thought of as either!'

'Poor Charly.' He caressed the hair at her temple, his expression indulgent.

She flinched from his touch. 'I'm not "poor" anything——'

'Oh yes, you are,' he nodded regretfully. 'You've had to be strong since your husband and daughter died. It's time you let someone else take charge for a while.'

'You?' she scorned.

'Me,' he confirmed arrogantly.

Her mouth twisted. 'When James died I swore no one else would ever "take charge" of my life,' she told him coldly. 'No one else ever has.'

'Until now.'

She looked at him with narrowed assessing eyes. 'I'll admit you're making a nuisance of yourself, but that's all you are doing.'

Aaron sighed. 'Is Matt the only man that can get through to you?'

'At the moment, yes.' Matt posed no threat, offered only friendship, a friendship she greatly valued.

He shrugged acceptance of the situation. 'The

way you said that tells me that it won't always be that way. And I can be very persistent.'

'I know that,' she said dryly.

'Will you drive me to my hotel; Erin and I came in a taxi.'

She sighed. 'Very well. And after this I don't want to see you again until next Friday,' she warned. 'No more popping up to my apartment when you feel like it, and no more friendly confidences to Molly about our future life together. Is that agreed?'

'What do I get out of the deal?'

She smiled. 'A lift back to your hotel.'

Aaron frowned. 'That doesn't seem a very fair deal on my side.'

'It isn't,' she acknowledged smoothly.

'Then what makes you think I'll agree to it?' he derided mockingly.

'It's almost impossible to get a taxi here this time of night, and it's just starting to rain?'

Appreciation for her show of humour shone in his eyes. 'That was pure Charly Allenby,' he grinned. 'And you have yourself a deal.'

She turned to him frowningly as they hurried to her car. 'I wish you would get the idea out of your head that I'm two different personalities.' She unlocked the door, both of them hurrying inside the car, the rain falling heavier now. 'I'm just me, Charly Hart.'

'You have never been "just" anybody in your life,' he mocked. 'What did I tell you?' he added with satisfaction.

'What——?' She followed his line of vision, just in time to see Bill and Erin crossing the car park to his car a short distance away. 'Her

brother won't mind about the owner of an
electronics company?' she derided, manoeuvring
her car out into the flow of slow traffic, visibility
poor.

'I won't tell him if she doesn't,' Aaron
dismissed. 'I'd offer to drive,' he murmured as
the traffic slowed almost to a stop, the rain, with
typical English weather unpredictability, turning
to hail, 'but I don't want to run the risk of being
called a chauvinistic pig again.'

She gave him a brief grin. 'Did I once call you
that?' she mocked.

'You know you did,' he said dryly.

She shook her head. 'I only called you a male
chauvinist, you added the pig. Why did you
follow me tonight, Aaron?' she asked abruptly.

'The truth?'

'I never ask for anything less,' she bit out
sharply.

'We have unfinished business,' he shrugged.
'I'm not about to let any other man collect on that.'

Her mouth tightened as she knew what
business he was referring to!

'Tell me, Charly.' He turned completely in his
seat to look at her. 'If Erin and I hadn't broken
up your evening would you have slept with Bill
Shaw tonight?'

'I don't have to answer that!' she snapped.

'You don't *have* to,' he agreed softly. 'But I'd
like you to.'

'I've already told you Bill is a business
acquaintance,' she dismissed.

'That doesn't answer my initial question,' he
pointed out determinedly.

'The truth?' she delayed.

Aaron nodded, his gaze compelling. '*I* never ask for anything less either.'

She moistened her lips, knowing he was stubborn enough to just keep asking until he got the answer he demanded. 'No,' she answered abruptly.

His breath left his body in a relieved sigh. 'Thank you.' His hand rested lightly on her thigh, gently caressing.

The now familiar heat coursed through her body at his touch, and she stiffened resentfully. 'Aaron——'

'No, don't spoil it,' he interrupted, his fingertips on her lips.

'I don't want you——'

'Please,' he instructed gently, turning her to face him as she stopped the car outside the front of his hotel. 'Good night, Lady,' he kissed her gently, getting out of the car to stand on the steps watching her as she accelerated away.

CHAPTER SEVEN

'You have to see that it's worth it, Ian.' She looked at the middle-aged man for his opinion.

He continued to look around the old stone building. 'Shevton's demands still seem excessive to me,' he finally commented.

Richard Shevton was now asking a ridiculous price for his old family home, both Charly and Aaron still determined to own it. As her lawyer and adviser Ian had questioned her need for this particular house, and she had brought him down here today to show him just how suitable it was for Matt's purposes.

Charly liked Ian, had always respected his opinion in the past, but she knew about this he was wrong. 'Pay him,' she instructed.

He shrugged. 'If you say so. But Grantley seems to be as determined as you are.'

She knew all about Aaron's determination, wasn't she fictitiously engaged to him because of that same determination to stop Matt making a fool of himself over her! 'The price now asked must be going past the realms of viability for the hotel he has in mind,' she dismissed. 'He'll have to back down soon.'

Ian sighed. 'The price has gone past the realms of viability for you too!'

She gave him an encouraging smile. 'You know as well as I do that I can go a lot higher before it even begins to hurt me.'

'That isn't the point——'

'The point is, Ian,' she cut in firmly, 'that I want Shevton House.'

'Unfortunately, so do I.'

They both turned simultaneously to face Aaron, leaning against the thick stone doorway as he made the statement. He looked so arrogantly confident, so condescending, that Charly knew he had once again misunderstood her motives, that he suspected her relationship with Ian now. He suspected her relationship with every man she even spoke to! Although perhaps that wasn't so surprising after the initial assumption he and Molly had both made about her staying at Matt's apartment.

'Aaron,' she greeted abruptly as he strolled towards them.

'The agent for the house told me you were here,' he drawled, looking at Ian with narrowed eyes. 'I assumed you were alone.'

Her mouth tightened. 'It's amazing how assumptions can so often be wrong.'

Green eyes hardened as he picked up her double meaning. 'Not always,' he muttered, putting out his hand to Ian, slightly taller than the lawyer, his dark blue suit and shirt perfectly tailored. 'Charly seems to have forgotten her expensively bought manners,' he bit out. 'I'm Aaron Grantley,' he introduced himself.

Ian was visibly startled, meeting the other man's hand cautiously as he murmured his own name.

'Ian is my lawyer,' Charly supplied irritably as Aaron continued to look at them speculatively.

His expression didn't change. 'Really?'

'Yes,' she snapped as he didn't even try to hide

his scepticism. 'He's the man who has been doing my negotiating for this house.'

'There always seems to be a man involved somewhere,' Aaron drawled.

Ian frowned at the insult. 'Now look here——'

'It's all right, Ian.' She put her hand on his arm. 'Perhaps you wouldn't mind waiting for me outside?' she suggested gently.

He looked from her to Aaron, and then back again, obviously not liking what he read from the other man's expression.

'Please, Ian,' she persuaded. 'I shouldn't be long.'

'Very well,' he agreed. 'I'll go through and have another look at the kitchens.'

Charly watched him go, knowing he resented being asked to leave. But Aaron was spoiling for a fight, and she didn't want Ian involved in that.

She turned to Aaron with snapping eyes, ignoring the fact that her senses had leapt when she first saw him, not having seen him for the last two days. 'Did you have to be so rude?' she demanded coldly.

'Rude?' he scorned. 'I haven't even started! Every time I look around there's a different man holding on to your skirt!'

Her eyes frosted over. 'Ian was James' lawyer, my father's and Will Hart's before that!'

'So?'

'So I've known him almost since I was in the cradle!'

'The man is forty-five years old at the most,' Aaron derided.

'Forty-four,' she corrected abruptly. 'And you just embarrassed him.'

'A little sensitive about your relationship, is he?' Aaron scorned. 'Is he another married one?'

She drew in an angry gasp. 'You——'

'Is he?' he demanded roughly.

'Ian is married,' she nodded. 'He is also the nearest thing to a best friend I've ever had!'

'Besides Matt,' Aaron's mouth twisted. 'Best friends are usually of your own sex.'

'So I'm unusual,' Charly snapped.

'You certainly are,' Aaron scorned harshly. 'You have the bedroom habits of a rabbit—anyone and everyone!'

She knew she paled, could feel the colour drain out of her cheeks. 'I didn't have you!' she spat out.

'And aren't I glad about that now,' he nodded. 'I'm a little more discriminating about my bed-partners!'

Each word was designed to wound, and if she really were the woman Aaron believed her to be maybe they would have done. As it was his insults were almost laughable. Even James, an expert in the art of deliberately hurting her, would never have accused her of being a sexual athlete, had known of her aversion to all men once he had finished humiliating her.

'Actually, so am I,' she told him coldly. 'Which is why *you've* never been invited into my bed.'

'I would never ask to be!'

'Good!'

She knew they must look and sound ridiculous as they glared mulishly at each other, but she also knew they were both too stubborn to back down. And despite his painful denial of desiring her she knew that Aaron did still want her; it was there in the heat of his emerald gaze, and the pulse throbbing in his jaw. If they weren't both aware of Ian's presence somewhere in the house they could have lain down on this cold stone floor and made love to each other right now! She was beginning to wonder why she had ever said no to this man.

'I'd better go,' she said jerkily, disturbed by her own thoughts. 'Will you lock up or shall we?'

'I'll do it,' he rasped, his jaw tight.

She nodded, walking away, tired suddenly, weary of answering this man's accusations.

'Charly . . .?'

She stiffened, looking at him with icy eyes. 'My name is Mrs Allenby-Hart,' she stated flatly. 'Or Rocharlle if you prefer.'

His mouth firmed. 'I wish I understood you,' he muttered.

'Maybe if you stopped thinking every man I'm with is a lover you might,' she said heavily.

'But there are so many of them,' he shook his head.

'All explainable.'

'Matt?'

'A friend.'

'Shaw?'

'Not even that.'

'Anderson?'

'My lawyer and friend.'

Aaron shook his head. 'No woman has that many male friends.'

'I do,' she sighed. 'But you obviously don't believe that, so let's end this conversation before you say anything I'll regret hearing. I'm sure you wouldn't regret saying it!'

'Maybe I would,' he muttered. 'But it wouldn't make it any less the truth.'

She gave him a pitying look before leaving him to join Ian, the other man taking one look at her face and wisely not saying another word until they were well on their way back to London.

'So that was Aaron Grantley,' he finally murmured.

She gave a choked laugh, still a little shaken by the unexpected encounter. 'Yes.'

Ian glanced at her, the two of them having driven down in his car. 'Does he always make snap judgments like that?' he drawled knowingly.

She shrugged. 'How would I know?'

'I just thought you might.'

'Well I don't,' she snapped.

'Charly, if the man is bothering you——'

'He isn't,' she dismissed tersely, knowing she lied. Aaron bothered her more than any other man she had ever known. But she was still afraid, so very afraid, of trusting her emotions again.

'Does it make you feel safer, emotionally, if you buy a man's affection?'

Charly recoiled from the accusation as Aaron forced himself into her apartment as soon as she opened the door. His words hit her like a physical blow.

He faced her angrily across the lounge. 'Does it?'

She swallowed hard. 'I don't know what you mean.'

'Then let me help you understand,' Aaron scorned harshly. 'Matt's apartment.'

She looked more puzzled than ever. 'What

about it? You know why I was staying there.' It was only yesterday she had had her last argument with him at Shevton House; she couldn't imagine what she had done to merit this second attack.

His mouth twisted. 'I also know now why that apartment was the obvious choice.'

She stiffened, her hands twisting together. 'I told you——'

'You've told me one load of garbage after another. You own this building, don't you?' he accused scathingly, very dark and attractive in faded denims and a thick black sweater, the sleeves of the latter pushed up to his elbows, his arms tanned and covered in fine hair.

Her head went back challengingly. 'And what if I do? There's no law that says I can't own an apartment building!' she snapped.

'You can own as many apartment buildings as you damn well please,' he bit out furiously. 'It's the men you keep in them that bothers me!'

'What on earth do you mean?' she demanded indignantly.

'Matt lives in this apartment building.'

'He occasionally sleeps here,' she corrected haughtily. 'He doesn't live here. But there's nothing wrong in that.'

'No,' he acknowledged scornfully. 'If he legitimately rented the apartment there wouldn't be.'

She swallowed hard, moistening suddenly dry lips. 'Of course he rents the apartment. He——'

'He pays no rent, Charly,' Aaron put in softly, challengingly.

'That's nonsense——'

'I checked,' he slowly shook his head. 'Only

two people in the building don't pay rent, you and Matt.'

'That's ridiculous,' she blustered. 'Of course he——'

'Don't lie to me, Charly.' Steel edged his voice. 'I may come over as an easygoing sort of guy.' He ignored her snort of disbelief. 'But I grew up in the tough streets of New York, and I grew tough with them.' His eyes were cold. 'But one thing I've always despised is liars. You're a liar, Rocharlle Hart,' he told her harshly. 'Matt stays here when he can get out of going home free, gratis, for nothing——'

'I do know the meaning of the words,' she snapped resentfully, wishing she knew who had told him that piece of confidential information. But he would never tell her, and she knew she would never be able to find out any other way. 'I just don't happen to consider it any of your business how Matt lives here.'

Many a night after spending time with her as she sat at Stephanie's bedside Matt had slept on a cot-bed a friend kept for him. It had been far from an ideal arrangement, and the strain often showed. She had moved into this apartment herself so that her home was near the hospital, rarely leaving Stephanie's side, but when she did not wanting to be away too long. An apartment on a lower floor had become vacant and she had offered it to Matt. Of course he had refused it, but when she had pointed out that he could let other colleagues in the same position use it he had reluctantly agreed to accept the use of it. But neither of them had ever thought their motives would be so misunderstood!

'I'm making it my business,' Aaron rasped. 'Molly won't be fooled for ever, you know. She believes that several of the doctors got together to pay for the rent on this place. It would break her up if she knew Matt was no more than a bought and paid for lover!'

Charly shook her head. 'You don't know what you're talking about.'

'Believe me, I know,' he bit out disgustedly. 'So answer my question, do you feel safer if you buy affection?'

'Get out of here!' she gasped. 'And take your filthy thoughts with you!'

'Can't you face the truth of what you're doing? Or have you always been like this?' he frowned. 'Did you buy yourself a husband too?'

'No!'

'I think you did.' His eyes glittered. 'You dangled your father's partnership with Hart's father in front of his nose to get him to marry you.'

'You have it all wrong—as usual,' she told him shakily.

'The man was years older than you——'

'Then he was also more experienced,' she pointed out heatedly. 'Do you honestly think an eighteen-year-old could seduce an experienced man of twenty-eight?'

'*You* could!'

'Thank you for your confidence,' she said wearily. 'But you have that the wrong way around. My husband was constantly unfaithful——'

'I know all about Hart's affairs.'

She sighed. 'You've been doing your homework.'

Aaron's mouth twisted. 'I've always believed in knowing all that I could about my adversaries.'

She frowned. 'We aren't enemies.'

'Oh yes, we are,' he nodded hardly. 'Because you're so damned beautiful I lost sight of my reason for knowing you at all for a while,' he rasped. 'But it's all clear to me now.'

'I wish it were to me,' she said wearily.

'It will be,' his voice was softly threatening. 'You may be discreet in your affairs, but once you look deeper than the surface beauty it becomes obvious just how many men you know. It was probably the reason your husband turned to other women.'

'Now listen here——'

'To more lies?' he scorned. 'The rumour is that your husband and daughter were leaving you at the time of the accident; as you were obviously unfit to be any child's mother he should have done it years before!'

Dry sobs wracked her body as she struck out at him blindly, pounding at him with her fists, unaware of the time the tears began to cascade down her cheeks, just hitting him over and over again, calling him every foul name James had ever called her, and a few more that he hadn't.

'Charly, for God's sake!' Aaron sounded exasperated as he warded off her hands, clasping her wrists as she didn't stop striking out at him. 'You're damned hysterical,' he rasped.

'I always get this way when I'm accused of being an unfit mother!' She was breathing heavily, hatred for him in her eyes. How dare he say she was unfit to be Stephanie's mother when she had suffered numerous humiliations just to stay close to her daughter?

'Do you deny that your husband was taking your daughter from you when they crashed?'

'I'm not denying or admitting anything to you,' she told him icily. 'Get out of my home and never come back.'

Uncertainty flickered in his eyes. 'Charly——'

'Get out,' she said again flatly.

'Maybe if we talked——'

'I have nothing to say to you.' She turned her back on him, willing him to leave before she broke down completely, the trembling beginning as soon as she heard the door close behind him.

She moved blindly across the room to the telephone, dialling before she had time to think. 'Ian?' She sighed her relief as he answered on the third ring. 'I know it's late—Yes, I'm fine,' she lied, her whole body shaking in reaction now. 'I hope I haven't disturbed you? Good,' she nodded as he assured her she hadn't, 'Ian, I want the Shevton House deal sewn up by the weekend. I don't care what you have to pay to get it but I want it to be mine by Friday afternoon at the latest.'

She stared sightlessly at the wall after the call had ended. The house would be hers, she would give it to Matt after he had spoken to Molly over the weekend—and then she never wanted to see Aaron Grantley again!

CHAPTER EIGHT

'AND this is where I keep the tea and coffee.' Molly closed the last cupboard in the kitchen. 'I think I've shown you where everything is.' She looked around the room frowningly.

'Including the sink,' Charly teased, being given a conducted tour before the other couple left on their weekend away.

Aaron was in the lounge with Matt, and Charly had been studiously avoiding any verbal or physical contact with him since he had arrived shortly after her an hour ago, their original plan to drive down together ignored by her; she couldn't have stood to be alone with him all that time! She had also ignored his numerous calls to her office the last week, not interested if he wanted to apologise, and not wanting to listen if he just wanted to throw out more accusations. He had refrained from coming to see her in person.

'Yes, well——' Molly looked embarrassed. 'I've never been away like this before.'

'You'll enjoy it,' she assured the other woman. 'I know it's no good me telling you not to worry about the children,' she had already spent a pleasurable hour with the two youngsters, 'because you will anyway,' she gently chided. 'But I can assure you they will be fine with me.'

'Are you and Aaron okay?' Molly frowned her concern.

'Of course.' She feigned surprise at the question.

'You both seem a little—distant.' Molly still looked worried.

Charly smiled reassuringly. 'We've both had a difficult week,' she understated, having had trouble getting through the latter part of hers. Although Aaron didn't seem to have had the same trouble, had looked just as relaxed and confident as usual when he arrived. 'Don't worry, we'll soon relax,' she told the other woman.

'Matt and I can always go away for this weekend some other time if you and Aaron need to——'

'Molly, will you stop worrying and take that gorgeous husband of yours away from here,' she teased.

Molly wrinkled her nose. 'I've got to the stage where I don't want to go.'

'I know,' Charly acknowledged gently. 'But by this time tomorrow you'll wonder what all the fuss was about.'

'You think so?' Molly didn't look convinced.

'I know so.' She firmly turned the other woman and pushed her out of the room in the direction of the lounge. 'Matt, take this wife of yours away for a romantic weekend before she decides she would rather stay here and change nappies.'

'Well, when you put it like that ...' Molly giggled, her arm about Matt's waist as he cuddled her to his side. 'I can't tell you how grateful we are to you.' She sobered. 'Maybe we can do the same for you one day?'

Charly's laugh was forced as she avoided looking at Aaron. 'Maybe,' she said non-committally.

She cuddled Tommy, and Aaron held Lucy aloft on his shoulders as they walked out to the car with the other couple.

'Now Tommy's spare nappies are in his cupboard upstairs, and if Lucy——'

'Molly, will you get in the car and just go,' Aaron drawled. 'Charly and I will cope.'

'Oh all right.' Molly glared at him as she got in the car and wound down the window. 'I'm only behaving like a mother, aren't I, Charly?'

'Yes.' She smiled to take the sharpness out of her reply, aware of green eyes on her. 'But I can assure you Tommy won't run around without a nappy, and Lucy won't go hungry.'

'She's such a finicky eater——'

'Molly, close the window and let's go.' Matt was ruefully impatient. 'Women!' he added indulgently.

'I'm only concerned——'

'Mummy, as soon as you've gone Aunt Charly is going to give us a bath,' Lucy told her mother primly.

Molly spluttered with laughter. 'Well that puts everything into perspective.' She kissed her daughter as Aaron held her up in front of the car window. 'Have a nice time, darling,' she choked before giving Tommy his kiss, waving at them out of the back window until the car disappeared out of sight.

'Okay,' Charly said briskly, seeing that now that their parents had actually gone the children weren't altogether sure they liked the idea, Tommy's bottom lip trembling precariously. 'Last one undressed and into the bath gets a sweet.' She took hold of Lucy's hand as Aaron put her down on the ground, running into the house and up the stairs to the bathroom with Tommy in her arms.

'You said the *last* one,' Lucy finally realised as she jumped naked into the warm water.

Charly laughed. 'So I did,' she teased.

'Then I must be the winner,' Aaron watched them from the open doorway as Tommy was gently placed in the bubble-topped water opposite his sister. He strolled further into the room. 'Do I get the sweet, Aunt Charly?'

She concentrated on washing the children. 'We all get one sweet after the bath,' she said flatly.

Lucy squinted up at him as Charly washed her silky hair. 'Are you really coming in the bath with us, Uncle Aaron?'

'Not this time,' he smiled. 'I might embarrass Aunt Charly.'

'Mummy and Daddy often get in the bath together,' the little girl told them candidly.

'Do they indeed?' Aaron said with mock seriousness, while Charly did her best to hold back a smile.

'They often get in with us too,' Lucy said with all the intensity of a five-year-old.

'How about it, Charly?' He quirked dark brows at her.

'No, thank you,' she refused primly, hearing how pompous she sounded but unable to do anything about it. She was going to find it difficult just being polite to Aaron this weekend, but she had been determined not to let Molly and Matt down. 'I bathed earlier,' she added stiltedly.

'Need any help here?' Aaron offered gently, seeming to sympathise with her awkwardness.

'No, thank you,' she refused again, still not looking at him.

'Then I'll go and see about getting dinner started.'

She turned sharply. 'I can get it!'

Green eyes held her gaze steadily, refusing to let her look away now that she had finally looked at him. 'We're in this together, Charly,' he told her softly. 'I wouldn't dream of letting you do all the work.'

'Don't you think I'm capable?' She couldn't help the sharpness of her tone, but luckily the children seemed too engrossed in the toys they had floating about on top of the water to take any notice of the adults' exchange.

'Charly——'

She turned away from the regret in his eyes. 'Molly left the food for dinner out in the kitchen. The steaks are ours,' she added dryly.

'With Tommy only having six teeth I would never have guessed,' Aaron derided.

She sighed. 'I'm sorry.'

'So am I. Charly, about the other night——'

She turned furious eyes on him. 'This is hardly the time or place to discuss it!'

'No,' he conceded heavily as Lucy looked up curiously. 'Later, then?'

'I don't think so.' She got Tommy out of the water, making him giggle as she dried him, ignoring the broodingly silent man across the room, aware of the exact moment he turned impatiently and went downstairs.

Whether it was the novelty of having Aaron and Charly in the house that made Lucy eat Charly didn't know, but the little girl ate quite a good meal. Aaron volunteered to put Tommy to bed while she took Lucy up, and although she offered to do it he insisted. Somehow the little joke she had intended playing on him concerning the baby no longer seemed appropriate and after settling Lucy down for the night, her well-worn teddy bear cuddled up against her, she went along the corridor to Tommy's bedroom. Surprisingly all was quiet inside.

The door was slightly ajar, and she pushed it open a little further, taking a few minutes to adjust her eyesight to the warm orange glow from the small night-light, making out a figure sitting in the rocking-chair in one corner, a blond head nestled against the darkness of Aaron's shirt. Aaron nodded as he stood up to put the baby in his cot; Charly hurried downstairs.

She was in the kitchen when she became aware that Aaron had joined her, the nervousness that she had been fighting all day creeping over her. 'Molly thought that was a secret,' she murmured, checking on the potatoes she had put on to cook.

'Singing Tommy to sleep?' He lounged against a cupboard. 'Matt found out about it a long time ago, but he didn't let Molly know he knew.'

'It would have ruined it for her,' Charly nodded.

'Yes. But Matt thought I ought to know about it.'

'I was just coming to tell you.'

'Charly, can't you even look at me?' he coaxed.

Her back stiffened. 'No,' she answered honestly.

'We can't go on like this,' Aaron sighed.

'No,' she acknowledged huskily.

'Charly——'

'I'm doing this for Molly and Matt.' She avoided his hands as he would have reached for her. 'There's nothing that says I have to enjoy it!'

'The children——'

'Will know no tension from me.' Her eyes were silver as she at last looked at him. 'I'm not as insensitive as you seem to think I am!'

'Charly, we have to talk about the other night,' he insisted firmly. 'Maybe we were a little hasty——'

'*I* wasn't the one that was hasty. And there was no maybe about it,' she told him coldly.

'After watching you with the kids tonight I think perhaps you're right,' he sighed wearily. '*I* was hasty. You obviously adore children and they adore you.'

She just looked at him, still too emotionally aroused by the accusations he had made concerning Stephanie, completely bewildered by the way she had totally lost control afterwards and beat at him with her fists; she had never done anything like that before, not even when she had first learnt of James' affairs.

'Charly, I'm sorry about what I said concerning your daughter.' He looked at her worriedly as she still didn't speak. 'Whatever your husband was doing with her that day I'm sure——'

'He was taking her away,' she revealed flatly. 'As you said he was.'

'I don't believe it—'

She gave a scornful laugh. 'Do you always react this way when told you were right?'

Aaron frowned. 'You weren't an unfit mother——'

'I didn't say I was,' she rasped. 'Just that James was taking Stephanie away from me.

'Why?'

'Dinner is ready,' she told him briskly.

'*Why*, Charly?' He grasped her arms, forcing her to look at him.

'He wanted a divorce.'

'And you wouldn't give him one?'

'No.'

'So he took your daughter away from you?'

She avoided his eyes. 'For good,' she said abruptly.

'I knew they both died in the accident but—Do you think he deliberately killed them both?' Aaron said disbelievingly.

She didn't correct the assumption he had made that Stephanie had died in the accident with James, those months of watching her daughter slowly die still too painful to talk about. 'I'm sure he didn't; he liked life too much for that.'

'Charly, will you talk to me?' Aaron requested softly. 'I have a feeling a lot of my other accusations could be explained away as easily,' he said self-derisively.

It would be so easy to talk to this man, to tell him everything, but her emotions were still bruised, her feelings for him still something she was frightened to acknowledge even to herself.

She looked at him coldly. 'I am not in the habit of explaining myself to anyone, and I'm certainly not going to start with you!'

He gave a pained wince. 'All right, Mrs Hart,' he drawled. 'I won't push you. But you—or Charly—will talk to me one day. And in the meantime I'm not going to jump to conclusions any more. I'm not naturally a jealous person,' he derided. 'It must be something you alone bring out in me.'

Jealousy? To feel jealousy surely he had to care? Did that mean she cared about him too; she had felt jealousy until she knew who Erin was!

'Would you watch the steaks for a moment?' she requested abruptly. 'I think I hear Lucy calling.'

Aaron frowned. 'I didn't hear anything.'

Neither had she, but she couldn't stay in the same room with him at this moment, was too shaken by the realisation that she *did* love this man!

But loving someone didn't solve any of the problems that love caused. She had loved once before, unhappily, and she had no reason to think it would be any different with Aaron, didn't think he was a better choice than James had been.

The trouble was she hadn't chosen to love Aaron. If she had had a choice it would be not to love any man ever again. She had known enough pain in her life already, and she had no reason to suppose loving Aaron would be any better than loving James.

She watched Aaron warily once she returned from seeing to a quite undisturbed Lucy, but he seemed determined to be charming, talking to her about his New York childhood, his happy homelife with his happily married parents.

She liked listening to him, and hadn't realised how late it was until he stood up stretching tiredly.

'It's been a long week,' he sighed at her questioning look.

'Please, go up to bed.' She stood up too. 'I'll just tidy our cups away.'

'Charly——'

She flinched as he touched her. 'I don't know what your plans were for tonight,' she rasped, 'but I hope they didn't include me.'

His mouth twisted. 'The trouble at the moment is that *all* of my plans include you,' he derided. 'Before I do anything I find myself asking "Will Charly like it?", "Will she approve?".'

The colour left her cheeks. 'I won't approve if you try to get me to go to bed with you.'

'I haven't said or done anything to imply I would do such a thing,' he chided.

'You haven't needed to!' she told him shakily. 'I can't, Aaron,' she choked.

'I know.' He touched her cheek gently. 'What woman could after the things I've said to you?'

'It isn't just that——'

'I do understand, Charly,' he assured her softly. 'Which is why I'm going up to bed now. Alone.'

She smiled her relief that he didn't try and force the matter, knowing that if he had she wouldn't have been able to resist.

'Which isn't to say I'm not going to kiss you good night,' he groaned, bending his head.

She was caught off-guard, her lips opening to his, her arms going slowly about his waist. It was a long drugging kiss of deep sensuality, and Charly felt herself sway slightly as he released her.

'Good night,' he said huskily, walking to the door. He turned before leaving. 'Congratulations on the Shevton House deal, by the way,' he told her admiringly.

She gave him a startled look as he strolled out of the room and up the stairs. Her acquisition of the property had been made final only that morning, but as the other interested party she felt sure Aaron had known about it almost immediately. And yet he had chosen not to mention it until now. Why now?

She followed him up the stairs, knocking on the door of the room Molly had told her had been made up for them, the room Matt had told her she could use further down the corridor. 'Aaron, I——' He had instructed her to enter after her knock, but she froze in the doorway; he must hold some sort of record for undressing, stark naked as he stood across the room from her, taking his time about picking up his brown robe and pulling it on. She swallowed hard, affected by the lithe beauty of his body in spite of herself. 'Why didn't you mention Shevton House earlier?' Her voice sounded slightly higher than it usually did.

He shrugged. 'There was nothing else to say about it; you got it.'

She looked at him warily. 'You aren't angry?'

'Business is business.' He shrugged again.

'Oh.' She frowned her consternation. 'Good night, then.'

'Good night,' he drawled.

Charly was still frowning as she reached her own room. The acquisition of Shevton House had seemed very important to him earlier in the week, that had been one of the reasons she had been determined to get a quick decision on the deal herself, and now Aaron acted as if he hadn't cared if he got it or not. Even loving him she didn't trust him.

CHAPTER NINE

SHE still didn't trust him the next day as he set out to be charming to both her and the children. He took them all shopping, then out to lunch, holding Tommy on his knee as he fed him the food he was able to eat.

Charly knew that to anyone looking at them they must look like a normal family out on a shopping trip. And the feeling filled her with disquiet. She didn't want a husband or a family again, and yet Aaron and the children made it seem possible.

'A good day, huh?' Aaron smiled as they sat down together for a few minutes after the children had been put to bed.

'You're very good with children,' she said non-committally.

'I love them,' he nodded.

'Lucy and Tommy are——'

'Not just Lucy and Tommy,' he shook his head. 'I love all kids.'

'Ah yes,' her mouth twisted. 'You told Molly we would have three or four!'

'And I intend to,' he nodded.

'Not with me,' she scoffed.

Aaron shrugged. 'With whoever I marry.'

'Don't you think you would have to discuss that with her first?' Charly bristled at his arrogance.

'Most women want children.'

'But most women would also like the choice about having them!'

'If I don't get married it won't really matter will it,' he dismissed.

She heartily disliked the thought of Aaron marrying or having any kind of permanent relationship with another woman. She had kept love out of her life for so long and now it was ripping her to pieces!

'How about you?' he eyed her curiously. 'Do you really not intend marrying again?'

'Maybe if the right man came along I might——' She broke off as she realised what she had said, shock widening her grey eyes.

'Charly—Damn,' Aaron scowled as the telephone began to ring. 'I bet it's Molly again to see if we've put the offspring to bed properly!' He reached for the receiver with a rueful shrug, Molly having telephoned four times this weekend already. 'Yes, Molly,' he raised his eyebrows at Charly, the two of them sharing a moment of laughter together.

Charly went into the kitchen to begin preparing their dinner while Aaron related all the details of the day to Molly. She kept herself busy, determinedly not dwelling on what she had said about marrying again. She almost had the meal ready by the time Aaron joined her ten minutes later.

'I'm sure not all mothers can be that concerned,' he grimaced.

She smiled. 'They are. I remember——' She broke off again in confusion. She never talked about her beloved daughter, the memories too painful!

'Yes?' Aaron prompted softly, his gaze compelling. 'Tell me about your daughter, Charly.'

'There's nothing to tell,' she said abruptly, carrying their dinner through to the dining-room, her appetite completely gone.

'She was part of you,' Aaron pursued relentlessly. 'There must be something to say.'

She swallowed hard, tears flooding her eyes. 'I—She was a lovely little girl,' she began again. 'She hadn't even begun to live.' Anger entered her voice, her body rigid with tension. 'That— that bastard——'

'James?'

'Yes,' she hissed, beyond thinking now, all the resentment and pain she had harboured towards James the last year released as the torrent of words flooded out. 'Give him Hartall Industries, he said,' she no longer even saw Aaron, locked in her own private hell, 'and he wouldn't fight to keep Stephanie. But I couldn't do that,' she told Aaron pleadingly. 'Hartall belonged to Stephanie, it was her inheritance. He wanted to divorce me and marry my cousin Jocelyn, but if they had had children Stephanie would have got nothing. I couldn't agree to disinheriting her,' she told Aaron again chokingly.

'So he took her.'

'Yes.' She shuddered as she remembered the horrific scene when James had taken Stephanie from her. 'He destroyed her because I wouldn't agree to what he wanted.'

'I thought you said it wasn't deliberate?'

'It wasn't,' she rasped. 'But he still killed her. She would never have been with him that day if he hadn't wanted to punish me.'

'Surely you would have got Stephanie if you had gone to court for her?' Aaron frowned.

'I was not an unfit mother——'

'I know that,' he soothed her. 'I know that, Charly,' he encouraged.

'I might have got custody of her,' she sighed. 'But then again I might not. James had always been a good father, and the courts always take that into consideration nowadays. But none of that really mattered, because James knew that I would never put it to the test, that I would give him everything just to get Stephanie back. I never had the chance,' she choked.

'Charly, it wasn't your fault,' Aaron told her softly.

She froze. 'What do you mean?' she rasped. 'Of course it wasn't my fault.'

'You blame yourself for what happened——'

'I do not!'

'And it's only natural that you feel partly responsible,' he continued remorselessly. 'You and James argued, he took Stephanie——'

'I do not blame myself——' She stopped as her voice broke emotionally, giving up all pretence as sobs wracked her slender body. 'God, yes I do!' she cried. 'I should have agreed to what he wanted, should have let him have Hartall, as long as he left Stephanie alone.' She spilled out the guilt that had been haunting her the last year, not questioning how Aaron knew of that guilt; he seemed to know things about her she wouldn't admit to herself!

'Charly, you have to stop blaming yourself,' he held her close against his chest, smoothing her hair with soothing motions.

'But I could have saved her!' she choked.

'You couldn't!' He crushed her to him. 'It was all an accident. James only meant to punish you a little by taking Stephanie, he didn't mean either of them to get killed. You *know* that!'

'Yes. But——'

'Honey, you can't go on giving yourself this punishment.' He looked down at her with gentle eyes. 'You can't continue to live behind that wall where you don't allow emotions to touch you. Charly, you have to allow *me* to touch you.'

She knew he didn't mean physically. 'No!' she recoiled.

'Lady, I understand why you've been acting the way you have, I even understand why you choose men like Matt and Anderson; neither of them are a threat to your real emotions. But *I'm* a threat, and I'm going to go on being one until you can accept that it's me you want.'

He still believed she was involved with Matt and Ian! He had guessed so much else about her, had even realised what no one else had——that she blamed herself for the accident that had taken Stephanie from her. And yet he still didn't realise that she had kept all men at a distance except him.

Before she could answer him there was a cry from upstairs. 'Tommy?' he frowned.

She shook her head, moving swiftly out of his arms. 'It's Lucy.' She ran up the stairs.

The little girl was sitting up in bed crying, seeming to cry even harder as Charly entered the room.

'Darling, what is it?' She cuddled the little girl to her, shooting a worried frown at Aaron as he stood in the doorway. 'Lucy?' she prompted gently.

'When are Mummy and Daddy coming home?' she sobbed.

'Soon,' she crooned, the novelty of having her parents away obviously having faded for Lucy.

'*When*?'

'Tomorrow. Lucy——'

'I want Mummy,' the little girl wailed.

'She'll be home tomorrow, darling,' Charly continued to hold her. 'I bet she'll bring you a present too.' She already knew Molly had bought the children a toy each.

Blue eyes widened, the tears ceasing although she continued to sob gently. 'You think so?'

'I'm sure of it,' she smiled warmly. 'Now what happened? Did you have a bad dream?'

'Yes,' the little girl mumbled into Charly's neck. 'Will you stay with me until I'm asleep?' she pleaded.

'Of course,' Charly assured her, looking ruefully at Aaron.

He nodded, quietly leaving the room before Lucy became aware of his presence.

She sat on the bed for over an hour, Lucy determined not to go back to sleep, forcing herself to stay awake every time she seemed in danger of drifting off to sleep. Charly sat with her patiently, had often done the same with Stephanie, leaving it ten more minutes or so even after she was sure Lucy had fallen asleep before leaving the room, not wanting to disturb the little girl.

Aaron was in the lounge when she got downstairs, a glass of whisky in his hand. 'All right now?'

'Yes.' She avoided his eyes. 'I'll go and clear away in the dining-room. Would you like me to make you something else?' Neither of them had eaten earlier!

'I've done it,' he told her abruptly. 'And I couldn't eat a thing.' He looked at her with dark eyes. 'You should have children of your own, Charly.'

'No——'

'*My* children,' he continued determinedly.

She paled, swallowing hard. 'You're talking of marriage?'

'Yes.' He looked at her steadily.

She moistened stiff lips. 'Are you asking me to marry you?'

'Yes.'

'Why?'

His mouth firmed. 'The usual reasons!'

'You would have to explain them to me,' she derided. 'My last marriage was made out of greed and convenience. And I don't mean mine,' she added hardly.

Aaron sighed. 'I only say those things because I resent every other man in your life, including your husband.'

'James used me, he didn't love me!'

'I'm learning that,' Aaron nodded. 'I'm slowly learning all the reasons why you're locked in behind your emotions. But I love you, Lady,' he told her intently. 'I love you and I want to marry you.'

Elation flared—and then died. 'You don't know me,' she stated flatly.

'I know more about you than you think,' he denied. 'I know that you love children, that you have compassion for other people, that you're loyal to your friends. I also know that when you feel like it you can throw all business caution out the window,' he taunted.

'If you're talking about Shevton House——'

'Oh I am,' he nodded. 'We both know you paid over the odds for what, to most people, would be a damned monstrosity.'

'Not to me,' she told him tightly.

'Or me,' he accepted. 'But its purchase became a personal vendetta as far as you were concerned, one you were determined to win.'

'And I have,' she challenged.

He shrugged. 'In part. You own the house—but you haven't got rid of me. That was the idea, wasn't it?'

She gave him a resentful glare. 'Don't be ridiculous——'

'Admit it, Charly, now that the weekend is almost over, the deal won, you hoped never to see me again.'

'I *won't* ever see you again,' she told him firmly.

'You'll see so much of me you'll wonder how you managed without me!'

Her mouth twisted. 'Trying to save me from myself and my impetuous ways?' she scorned.

He shook his head slowly. 'There's nothing impetuous about you.'

'You might be surprised,' she said bitterly. Loving this man was pure madness! And she *daren't* even begin to believe he loved her in return.

'Lady, surprise me,' he invited huskily.

She was tempted, her senses jumping at the

thought of being in this man's arms. And maybe if they could just have gone to bed together it would be worth it. But Aaron was asking for so much more from her, and if she gave it she was afraid he would guess how she felt about him.

He sighed. 'I wish that hesitation didn't mean no.'

'And if it didn't?' she said recklessly, the force of her need taking over from caution.

His gaze probed hers. 'I'd carry you off to bed right now.'

She swayed with the force of her desire for this man. 'It doesn't mean no, Aaron,' she groaned.

His eyes darkened questioningly until he read from her expression that she was past fighting him. He took a step forward, not quite touching her but close enough for her to feel the seduction of his masculine warmth. 'You're sure?' he murmured.

She gave a choked laugh. 'Never ask a woman if she's sure, especially a confused one like me! I'm not sure about anything any more, Aaron.' She fell into his arms. 'But I do know I want you to make love to me.'

'It's a start,' he groaned as he bent his head, his lips claiming hers.

Charly deliberately blocked all other thoughts but this moment from her mind, meeting the devouring passion of his kiss, returning the thrust of his tongue, purring deep in her throat as he loosened her hair to press his fingers into her scalp.

By mutual consent they turned and walked up the stairs together, Aaron slowly undressing her once they reached the bedroom, his gaze never leaving her as he stripped off his own clothes. He didn't touch her except with his magnetic green gaze, her nipples filling and hardening to peaks, a heated warmth between her thighs.

'I know this is the part where I'm supposed to throw you on the bed and make love to you until you're senseless,' he drawled. 'But I don't want to rush this.' He took her hand in his. 'And I have a yearning to see all that golden hair slicked down your body, to lick the droplets of water from your breasts, to——'

'If you're suggesting we take a shower together then let's do it.' Her breathing was constricted with desire.

He laughed softly as they stepped under the hot spray of water, beginning to slowly wash every inch of her body. Charly was trembling uncontrollably by the time he reached her torso, her whole body tingling for his caresses, meeting his mouth hungrily.

'Aaron . . .!' she moaned longingly, excitement burning in her veins. 'I want you!'

'I know, Lady,' he breathed ruefully. 'Let's get out of here.' He turned the water off abruptly, making no move to pick up any of the towels on the rails, their inner heat drying their bodies within minutes as they lay down on the bed together.

'You're beautiful, Lady.' He touched her body almost reverently.

'I've had a child.' She knew she had the marks of that pregnancy on her body.

'It only makes you more beautiful.' He moved to kiss the tiny silver marks on her stomach. 'Will you have my children?'

'Aaron, please———!' she groaned as he found and explored the most sensitive part of her body. 'Now isn't the time to discuss children.'

'Perhaps not,' he conceded as he moved back up her body to kiss her on the mouth. 'But we will talk about it tomorrow,' he promised.

As the fire spread through her body, their caresses fevered, tomorrow seemed a long way off.

Aaron caressed and touched her until she felt on the edge of insanity, moving restlessly beneath him as she felt the probe of his hard desire against her thighs, his hair-roughened skin an eroticism in itself as he denied her full possession.

She almost went over the edge of her desire as he gently opened her thighs to enter her, her tightness closing about him moistly, the slight initial discomfort soon forgotten as Aaron began to move slowly inside her.

He continued to move slowly even though she begged for release, her fingers digging into the taut skin of his back, her mouth meeting his hungrily as her head came up to meet his, groaning her satisfaction as he quickened his pace, thrusting deeper and deeper inside her as she arched up in spiralling completion, wave after wave of pleasure shuddering through her body, her gasped cries turning to ones of triumph.

Aaron held her as the tremors continued to shake her body, her starved lungs gasping for air, clinging to his shoulders as she buried her face against his throat.

'You haven't—You didn't——'

'I'm going to,' he assured her throatily. 'I had

to make it good for you first.'

As he slowly began to move inside her once again Charly knew a moment's surprise as she felt the heat rising within her once again, and then she gave herself up to the sensation of pleasing Aaron so that he couldn't hold back any more, going up in the clouds with him again herself.

They didn't speak afterwards as they lay with Charly's head on his shoulder, but there was no awkwardness between them as they drifted off to sleep together.

Charly was in the kitchen supervising the children's breakfast when Aaron put in an appearance the next morning, and she met his rueful smile shyly, having left him in bed still sleeping half an hour ago, not wanting to disturb him.

'Coffee?' he asked as he moved to the pot to pour some for himself.

'Not just now, thanks.' She turned back to feeding Tommy as he banged on the top of his high-chair impatiently. 'Tommy's hungry,' she derided, spooning more cereal into his waiting mouth.

'We're late,' Lucy put in disapprovingly.

Charly glanced at Aaron again as he leant against the cooker drinking his coffee. 'Yes, we are,' she murmured, unable to read anything from Aaron's expression. She needed his reassurance, but she realised that he was leaving the next move—if there were one!—up to her.

'You're even later than us.' Lucy looked at Aaron accusingly, obviously his sleeping in until ten o'clock not suiting her at all.

'I'm older than you are,' he excused, sitting

down at the table with them. 'How are you this morning, Charly?' he watched her intently.

'Is Aunt Charly ill?' Lucy looked up frowningly.

Aaron looked at her questioningly too, and she moistened her lips nervously as she realised he was giving her an opening for that 'move'. 'I was, Lucy,' she answered the child but looked at Aaron as she acknowledged that fact. 'But I think I'm getting better.'

Aaron seemed to visibly relax, his hand covering hers as it rested on the table. 'I hope so,' he said huskily.

She turned away awkwardly, covering her embarrassment by feeding Tommy. It was true, she had been ill, with a sickness of the heart. James had hurt her and humiliated her until she closed herself in from people. But loving Aaron had knocked down those barriers.

'We have to talk,' she told him as Lucy and Tommy dragged him out to the garden after breakfast.

'Tonight,' he promised as he was pulled out the door.

She was in love, as she had never loved James, and if Aaron were willing to take a risk on her she would do the same with him. Aaron had shown her in every way that he could that he loved her, even that hurtful jealousy. She had to put irrational uncertainties behind her, had to stop thinking of herself as unworthy of being loved just because James hadn't been able to love her. But she and Aaron also had a lot of things to talk about before they made any decisions about a future together.

*　　*　　*

Molly looked glowing as she stepped out of the car, laughing happily as Lucy and Tommy ran down the steps to greet them, bending down to hug them both before they ran over to their father.

'I think we'll have to go away more often.' Matt carried a child in each arm as he and Molly walked up the steps to the front door.

'Charly, it's wonderful, simply wonderful!' Molly hugged her, tears in her eyes. 'I don't know how we can ever thank you.'

'Hey, I had a hand in it too,' Aaron pretended indignation at being excluded.

Charly had stiffened at Molly's effusive thanks, and as the other woman looked puzzled by Aaron's statement she knew she had reason to be worried.

'You did?' Molly frowned at him. 'Matt?' she looked at her husband.

He slowly bent to put the children down, grimacing apologetically at the rigid-faced Charly. 'I think the two of you are talking at cross-purposes,' he murmured.

'We are? Oh.' Molly's brow cleared. 'Of course I'm very grateful to you for taking care of the children for us this weekend, Aaron,' she nodded. 'But I was talking about the house earlier. About Charly buying it to turn into a hospital.'

Charly looked anxiously at Aaron, cringing at the guarded look that came over his face.

'Oh yes?' he prompted non-committally.

Molly gave Charly another glowing smile. 'It's the most wonderful opportunity for Matt,' she said happily, looking at her husband proudly.

She forced herself to speak normally, although she was very aware of Aaron's narrow-eyed look. 'I take it you approve?' she teased the other woman.

'Of course,' Molly laughed dismissively, putting her hand in the crook of Matt's arm. 'It's what he's always wanted, but we would never have had the money for such a project,' she said regretfully.

'We were worried in case you couldn't cope, with the new baby coming along.' Still she avoided looking at Aaron.

'I'll cope,' Molly said determinedly. 'Isn't it marvellous, Aaron?'

Charly tensed as she waited for his response, her gaze fixed firmly on the carpet.

'Marvellous,' he finally agreed, moving forward to shake the other man's hand. 'Shevton House is very suitable for a hospital, and so convenient for you being only a short distance from here. This way you'll still be able to have the best of both worlds.'

Charly paled as he repeated everything she and Matt had said about the house when she had invited Matt to go down and look at it! But did he mean the praise as innocently as she and Matt had done, or did he still think she was trying to buy the affection of the other man?

CHAPTER TEN

'EXACTLY,' Molly agreed enthusiastically. 'Now let's all have a nice cup of tea and the children can open their presents.'

It wasn't until they were all seated in the lounge with their cups of tea, the children on the floor playing with their new toys, that Charly dared glance at Aaron again. What she saw frightened her. He looked cold and distant, his eyes hard, his mouth tight. He did believe she was still trying to buy Matt!

'I think it's time I left.' She stood up jerkily. 'I have a thousand things to do before going to work tomorrow,' she added lightly, wondering if she sounded as falsely bright as she felt.

'Oh, we thought you would both stay to dinner.' Molly looked disappointed.

'Not this time,' Charly refused regretfully—knowing there would never be another time.

'No, I'm afraid we have to be going,' Aaron stood up too.

Charly looked at him sharply—and then wished she hadn't. When she looked at him, seeing him as remote as that first evening they met, she knew she had lost him. 'There's no need for you to leave too—darling,' she added the endearment to take the sting out of her words, conscious of the fact that on Friday Molly had already believed things to be strained between them. Aaron could tell the other woman of the end of their relationship some other time! 'After all, we each have a car here.'

He met her gaze steadily. 'I have to leave now, anyway. I have some things to sort out in London myself.'

She paled slightly at the warning in his voice, turning away. 'I'll just go and get my case and bag.'

'I'll help you,' Matt offered before Aaron had the chance to do so.

She gave him a grateful smile. 'Thank you.'

Matt waited until they were in her bedroom before speaking. 'I'm sorry about that,' he grimaced.

'Don't be,' she dismissed reassuringly. 'If I were in Molly's position I wouldn't be able to stay quiet either.'

'I forgot to ask her not to say anything in front of anyone,' he admitted ruefully.

'I doubt if she would have thought that included Aaron anyway,' she derided.

Matt frowned. 'Have the two of you argued? You seem very on edge with each other.'

'Everything has gone very smoothly.' She picked up her bag to hide her flushed cheeks. 'And Shevton House is finally yours,' she told him with satisfaction as she followed him out of the room and down the stairs.

Excitement brightened his eyes. 'That's wonderful!'

She nodded. 'I'll call you towards the end of the week and make the necessary arrangements.'

'But not Friday,' Aaron put in softly, he and Molly standing in the hallway.

Charly swallowed hard, looking at him warily. 'Why not Friday?'

He didn't answer her, turning to look down at Molly. 'I forgot to mention it earlier, but Charly and I have decided on the date for our wedding.'

'Not—not *Friday*?' Molly sounded astounded.

'Why not?' he returned mildly.

'Well because—because——' She looked desperately at Charly. 'Tell him it isn't time enough to get ready for a church wedding!'

Charly had turned to ice at the mention of a wedding, knowing that Aaron had decided that now, more than ever, Matt needed saving from himself.

'We've decided to scrap the church idea,' Aaron told the other woman briskly, kissing her on the cheek before shaking Matt's hand. 'I can't wait any longer than Friday. Come on, honey.' He took a firm hold of Charly's arm and guided her towards the door.

She felt numb as they walked over to their cars, knowing that last night had meant nothing to Aaron after all.

'Aren't you going to say something?' he prompted gently as they reached her car. 'I realise I was high-handed in announcing we were getting married like that, but——'

'I understand your reason,' she told him woodenly.

He frowned. 'Then why can't you look at me?'

She did look at him then, the pain etched into her face. 'Trust is a fragile thing, Aaron, but last night I trusted you. It's a pity you can't do the same.'

'What are you talking about?' he shook his head.

She threw her case in the back of her car. 'I

would have thought by now you would have realised I have no designs on your friend,' she sighed.

'But I do realise that,' he told her unhesitatingly. 'I knew last night that you and Matt have never been lovers.'

'Then why——'

'Which one of them survived the crash, Charly?' he asked gently. 'It must have been Stephanie, you would never have felt this way if it were James.'

She was very pale. 'How did you know?' she asked in a hushed voice.

He shrugged. 'After Molly dropped her bombshell I tried to put two and two together without making my usual five. Was it Stephanie Matt tried to save?'

'Yes,' she confirmed chokingly.

He nodded. 'I'm going to follow you back to your apartment,' he told her firmly. 'Where we are going to clear up these misunderstandings once and for all. Then we are going to plan our wedding for Friday.'

Her eyes widened. 'You were serious about that?'

'Well, I did propose last night, and although I didn't actually receive a verbal reply I believe our actions afterwards were enough of an acceptance,' he mocked indulgently.

She blushed as she remembered the times in the night that they had turned to each other. 'Aaron——'

'Sweetheart, we can't talk here.' The gentle rebuke reminded her they were still standing in Molly and Matt's driveway. 'I'll follow you to your home. And please drive carefully,' he added tensely.

She knew how he felt, could feel herself on the edge of happiness, and was so afraid it was going to be taken from her. As it had so often in the past!

'Charly.' He touched her cheek lovingly. 'I'm going to be around for the next fifty or sixty years.'

She smiled tearfully at his ability to guess what was troubling her. 'Is that all?'

'Well I did once have a great-aunt that lived to one hundred and three. I suppose I could try and match that.'

'Please,' she smiled at him between her tears.

He put a hand either side of her face, cupping her cheeks. 'I love you, Charly Hart.'

'I—I——'

'You can do it, Charly,' he encouraged.

She smiled shakily. 'I love you, Aaron Grantley.'

He chuckled triumphantly. 'It will get easier with time.' He kissed her achingly. 'Drive carefully, but *fast*, hmm?' Desire gleamed in his eyes.

She drove badly and slowly, realising after she almost knocked one poor man off his bike that her concentration wasn't as good as it could have been, and that if she wanted them both to get back to London in one piece she had better calm down.

But she couldn't help the exhilaration she felt, sure that everything was going to work out.

As soon as her apartment door closed they fell into each others' arms, their mouths meeting hungrily, as if they had been parted for days and not minutes.

'Enough, woman.' Aaron finally put her away from him, his breathing ragged, his eyes dark. 'Stop trying to seduce me!'

She gave a splutter of laughter, questioning who had been seducing who!

'God, you're beautiful when you laugh.' His arms closed about her as he crushed her to him. 'I want you to laugh a lot when we're married,' he told her intently. 'I want you to be so happy you can't *stop* laughing!'

She clung to him, so happy *now* she didn't think she could be any happier.

'Now, we're going to talk.' He held her firmly away from him. '*I'll* talk,' he told her. 'You interrupt me if I go wrong. Okay?'

She was too full of emotion to want to talk now, and he knew it.

They sat down on the sofa together, Aaron's arm about her shoulders as he began to talk. 'After your parents died you were lonely and confused, James Hart took advantage of that loneliness and married you to gain full control of Hartall Industries.'

'I thought I loved him,' she admitted huskily.

'You mean he *wanted* you to think that,' Aaron corrected grimly. 'It wasn't a happy marriage——' He looked down at her questioningly as she made a murmur of protest. 'Correction, it did have one happy aspect,' he said gently. 'Stephanie. After years of indulging himself in fleeting affairs Hart decided he wanted to marry your cousin. But he didn't want to lose the company, not even a part of it, considered it

belonged to him now. And so he used the love he
knew you had for Stephanie to put pressure on
you to agree to his terms. We both know what
happened when you refused.' His arm tightened
about her. 'Stephanie was ill in hospital for a long
time——'

'Two months,' she confirmed heavily.

'You and Matt became friends during that
time,' he nodded. 'He was Stephanie's doctor,
wasn't he?'

She turned and buried her face in his chest.
'She never regained consciousness.'

'My poor love!' He crushed her to him. 'It was
because you saw how Matt cared, how much he
wanted Stephanie to live and get well, that you
decided to provide him with a hospital that
would specialise only in such patients. For
months you looked for the right building,
somewhere big enough to be a hospital, but
comfortable enough for those patients to regard it
as home while they recovered——'

'How did you know that?' she gasped.

'I know you, my darling,' he smiled. 'I also
know Matt's opinion of nursing such patients.
But once you found Shevton House you found
you had a rival for its purchase, an arrogant son-
of-a-bitch whose thoughts of you were usually in
the sewer!'

'Aaron——'

'I don't blame you for not wanting me to know
why you wanted Shevton House,' he assured her.
'Even loving you as I do, before last night I
would probably have suspected your motives.'

'I thought you did anyway,' she admitted
chokingly.

'I know you did,' he nodded. 'But after last night——'

'What was so special about last night?'

He looked down at her mockingly. 'You mean you don't know?'

Colour darkened her cheeks. 'Well of course I *know*. But——'

'Sweetheart, last night you gave yourself to me time and time again, exposed your inner emotions and needs, something I knew you would never do unless you loved me. Also, I made love to a woman who hadn't been made love to in a very long time—if ever. Oh, I know you slept with your husband, you had Stephanie, after all. But it wasn't what we had together last night.'

'No,' she acknowledged openly.

'Last night was love, for both of us. And so when Molly thanked you for giving Matt the chance to have his own hospital to specialise in I knew it had nothing to do with a close relationship between the two of you. For a while I was a little puzzled, but once I'd realised *which* house it was you were giving to Matt I worked it all out.' He grimaced. 'So much for my idea of it being a love-nest for the two of you! I have to admit I was a little put out at first that you hadn't trusted me with the truth, but once I thought about that some more I asked myself why the hell should you? Here was a woman who had been used and abused by one man, who had little reason to trust anyone, so why should she trust a man who does nothing but insult her!'

'I do trust you, Aaron.'

'Then it's about time I started earning that trust!'

'Darling, it wasn't your fault.' She touched his cheek lovingly. 'I could have cleared up many of our misunderstandings if I had cared to. But I didn't want to become involved again, so I deliberately let you think the worst of me. And then once I realised I loved you it seemed almost too late to put things right.'

'It will never be too late between us,' he told her forcefully. 'Although we are going to have to start confiding things to each other a bit more.'

'About Friday——'

'Yes?' He tensed.

She gave him a glowing smile. 'Can't we make it any sooner?'

'Lady!' His eyes darkened. 'As far as I'm concerned we've been married since last night.'

It was the way she felt too, knew that they had become two parts of a whole last night when they had given themselves to each other time and time again.

'Are you sure you won't mind having a working wife?' she asked tentatively.

'I wouldn't have it any other way,' he answered instantly.

She should have known that would be his answer. Aaron was a man who would never suppress or suffocate her, who would just love her for what she was.

'You were the one who said "now isn't the time to be talking about children",' Aaron reminded her anxiously.

Charly rested between the strong contractions, the two of them having arrived at the hospital just over three hours ago, she insisting on leaving it until the last minute before coming in.

It wouldn't be long now before their baby was born, and then Aaron would quickly forget all the worry he was feeling now. 'Darling—' she broke off as another contraction gripped her, squeezing his hand until his fingers looked bloodless, although he didn't make a move of protest, sharing her pain. The contraction had been even stronger this time, quicker too; it wouldn't be long now. 'I didn't mean for us not to think about them *at all*,' she teased.

Almost nine months after their wedding their first child was being born, and both of them were convinced it had been conceived that weekend at Molly and Matt's. Aaron had been actively involved in the preparations for the birth and afterwards since the beginning, but none of the classes they had attended together seemed to have prepared him for this moment.

She gasped as another contraction gripped her, knowing the birth was imminent as it went on and on, doing her best to help their child make its entrance into the world, feeling the exhilarating relief as the baby was born in a sudden rush of activity, the look on the doctor's face enough to tell her everything was all right with the baby.

'It's a boy, Charly,' Aaron choked as he stood up to look at his son. 'My God, it's a boy!'

She smiled through her exhaustion, sitting up enough with Aaron's help to look at her son for the first time. He was smoothly round, had a beautiful face, and a shock of golden hair.

'A healthy seven pounds four ounces,' the

nurse told her as she handed the blanket-wrapped baby to Charly.

She held the baby to her gently, slightly shaky still from the birth, awed by the perfection of her son. 'He's beautiful,' she said tearfully.

'Almost as beautiful as his mother.' Aaron's own cheeks were damp as she handed the baby to him. 'Daniel Aaron Matthew Grantley,' he murmured softly, the baby asleep in his arms. 'Quite a mouthful for such a little man.'

'He'll grow into it.' Charly smiled, moved by how deeply she loved this man and was loved in return by him, and how much they would both love their son. The nine months of their marriage had been happy ones—more than happy, *ecstatic*! She hadn't believed there could be such happiness. Daniel made everything perfect.

'Congratulations,' the doctor smiled. 'I'll see you again next year,' he teased before leaving.

'Like hell he will!' Aaron rasped.

Charly smiled tiredly. 'I thought you wanted three or four?'

'I've changed my mind.' He handed Daniel back to the nurse to be washed, holding Charly's hand. 'I had no idea what you would have to go through.' A frown marred his brow. 'Daniel is enough for me.'

'I don't believe in only children,' she teased.

'We'll borrow Lucy, Tommy, and Sara for weekends,' he answered instantly. 'They can keep Daniel company.'

'Coward,' she laughed softly.

His hand tightened on hers. 'How could you want to go through that again?'

'Quite easily,' she said ruefully.

'We'll talk about it once you're stronger,' he compromised.

'Just talk about it?' she teased.

'Nurse, are all new mothers as sexy as this?' He turned to the other woman, Daniel all snuggled down in the clear-sided crib.

She laughed. 'Only when they have husbands as handsome as you!'

Charly joined in the laughter as *he* was the one to look embarrassed. 'I love you, Aaron Grantley.'

'I love *you*, Charly Grantley. We finally got the name right,' he said with satisfaction.

She felt her lids begin to droop tiredly. 'Charly Grantley does sound rather nice.'

'I thought so,' he nodded smugly.

'Perfect . . .' She fell asleep, her *world* perfect at last.

Coming Next Month in Harlequin Presents!

863   MATCHING PAIR   Jayne Bauling
A lounge singer and a hotel owner are two of a kind. He chooses to live life on the surface; she feels she has no choice. Neither have been touched by love.

864   SONG OF A WREN   Emma Darcy
Her friend and lodger, a terrible tease, introduces her to his family in Sydney as his "live-in lady." No wonder his brother deliberately downplays their immediate attraction.

865   A MAN WORTH KNOWING   Alison Fraser
A man worth knowing, indeed! An English secretary decides that an American author is not worth getting involved with...as if the choice is hers to make.

866   DAUGHTER OF THE SEA   Emma Goldrick
A woman found washed ashore on a French Polynesian island feigns amnesia. Imagine her shock when her rescuer insists that she's his wife, the mother of his little girl!

867   ROSES, ALWAYS ROSES   Claudia Jameson
Roses aren't welcome from the businessman a London *pâtisserie* owner blames for her father's ruin. She rejects his company, but most of all she rejects his assumption that her future belongs with him.

868   PERMISSION TO LOVE   Penny Jordan
Just when a young woman resigns herself to a passionless marriage to satisfy her father's will, the man in charge of her fortune and her fate withholds his approval.

869   PALE ORCHID   Anne Mather
When a relative of his wrongs her sister, a secretary confronts the Hawaiian millionaire who once played her for a fool. She expects him to be obstructive—not determined to win her back.

870   A STRANGER'S TOUCH   Sophie Weston
One-night stands are not her style. Yet a young woman cannot deny being deeply touched by the journalist who stops by her English village to recover from one of his overseas assignments.

WORLDWIDE LIBRARY IS YOUR TICKET TO ROMANCE, ADVENTURE AND EXCITEMENT

Experience it all in these big, bold Bestsellers— Yours exclusively from WORLDWIDE LIBRARY WHILE QUANTITIES LAST

To receive these Bestsellers, complete the order form, detach and send together with your check or money order (include 75¢ postage and handling), payable to WORLDWIDE LIBRARY, to:

In the U.S.
WORLDWIDE LIBRARY
Box 52040
Phoenix, AZ
85072-2040

In Canada
WORLDWIDE LIBRARY
P.O. Box 2800, 5170 Yonge Street
Postal Station A, Willowdale, Ontario
M2N 6J3

Quant.	Title	Price
_____	**WILD CONCERTO**, Anne Mather	$2.95
_____	**A VIOLATION**, Charlotte Lamb	$3.50
_____	**SECRETS**, Sheila Holland	$3.50
_____	**SWEET MEMORIES**, LaVyrle Spencer	$3.50
_____	**FLORA**, Anne Weale	$3.50
_____	**SUMMER'S AWAKENING**, Anne Weale	$3.50
_____	**FINGER PRINTS**, Barbara Delinsky	$3.50
_____	**DREAMWEAVER**, Felicia Gallant/Rebecca Flanders	$3.50
_____	**EYE OF THE STORM**, Maura Seger	$3.50
_____	**HIDDEN IN THE FLAME**, Anne Mather	$3.50
_____	**ECHO OF THUNDER**, Maura Seger	$3.95
_____	**DREAM OF DARKNESS**, Jocelyn Haley	$3.95

	YOUR ORDER TOTAL	$_____
	New York and Arizona residents add appropriate sales tax	$_____
	Postage and Handling	$___.75
	I enclose	$_____

NAME _____

ADDRESS _____ APT.# _____

CITY _____

STATE/PROV. _____ ZIP/POSTAL CODE _____

WW3

What the press says about Harlequin romance fiction...

"When it comes to romantic novels...
Harlequin is the indisputable king."
— *New York Times*

"...always with an upbeat, happy ending."
— *San Francisco Chronicle*

"Women have come to trust these
stories about contemporary people,
set in exciting foreign places."
— *Best Sellers*, New York

"The most popular reading matter of
American women today."
— *Detroit News*

"...a work of art."
— *Globe & Mail*, Toronto

What readers say about Harlequin romance fiction...

"I absolutely adore Harlequin romances! They are fun and relaxing to read, and each book provides a wonderful escape."
—N.E.,* Pacific Palisades, California

"Harlequin is the best in romantic reading."
—K.G.,* Philadelphia, Pennsylvania

"Harlequins have been my passport to the world. I have been many places without ever leaving my doorstep."
—P.Z.,* Belvedere, Illinois

"My praise for the warmth and adventure your books bring into my life."
—D.F.,* Hicksville, New York

"A pleasant way to relax after a busy day."
—P.W.,* Rector, Arkansas

*Names available on request.

Can you keep a secret?

You can keep this one plus 4 free novels

PASSIONATE!
CAPTIVATING!
SOPHISTICATED!

Harlequin Presents...

**The favorite fiction
of women the world over!**

Beautiful contemporary romances that
touch every emotion of a woman's heart—
passion and joy, jealousy and heartache...
but most of all...love.

Fascinating settings in the exotic
reaches of the world—
from the bustle of an international capital
to the paradise of a tropical island.

**All this and much, much more
in the pages of**

Harlequin Presents...

Wherever paperback books are sold, or through
Harlequin Reader Service

In the U.S.
2504 West Southern Avenue
Tempe, AZ 85282

In Canada
P.O. Box 2800, Postal Station A
5170 Yonge Street
Willowdale, Ontario M2N 6J3

**No one touches the heart of a woman
quite like Harlequin!**

P-111

You're invited to accept 4 books and a surprise gift **Free!**

Acceptance Card

Mail to: Harlequin Reader Service®

In the U.S.
2504 West Southern Ave.
Tempe, AZ 85282

In Canada
P.O. Box 2800, Postal Station A
5170 Yonge Street
Willowdale, Ontario M2N 6J3

YES! Please send me 4 free Harlequin Romance® novels and my free surprise gift. Then send me 6 brand new novels every month as they come off the presses. Bill me at the low price of $1.65 each ($1.75 in Canada)—an 11% saving off the retail price. There are no shipping, handling or other hidden costs. There is no minimum number of books I must purchase. I can always return a shipment and cancel at any time. Even if I never buy another book from Harlequin, the 4 free novels and the surprise gift are mine to keep forever.

116 BPR-BPGE

Name _____ (PLEASE PRINT)

Address _____ Apt. No. _____

City _____ State/Prov. _____ Zip/Postal Code _____

This offer is limited to one order per household and not valid to present subscribers. Price is subject to change.

ACR-SUB-1

Experience the warmth of ...

Harlequin Romance

**The original romance novels.
Best-sellers for more than 30 years.**

Delightful and intriguing love stories
by the world's foremost writers
of romance fiction.

Be whisked away to dazzling
international capitals ...
or quaint European villages.
Experience the joys of falling in love ...
for the first time, the best time!

Harlequin Romance

A uniquely absorbing journey
into a world of superb romance reading.

**No one touches the heart of a woman
quite like Harlequin!**

R-111R